"A four-star, five-course, [...] has cooked up a delici[...] [...] characters, stirred them up with zany adventures and seasoned them thoroughly with tongue-in-cheek wit. It's a fine treat for mystery lovers, food and wine buffs or anyone who just wants to sit back and chuckle. . . . Bond is internationally and affectionately known as the author of the Paddington Bear series. But *Monsieur Pamplemousse* is as unlike a children's book as it is unlike a cookbook; it is a ribald, wacky whodunit, liberally spiced with culinary charm and served with a farcical flair."

Napa Register

"The pace remains madcap. . . . Pamplemousse is intrepid and hilarious. The descriptions of food are detailed, mouth watering and very French. It is hoped that Pamplemousse's first appearance will not be his last."

Portsmouth (New Hampshire) *Herald*

"Fans of the author's wryly amusing children's books featuring his now-famous Paddington Bear will be delighted to find that Bond has created a mad romp that is strictly for adults . . . side splitting."

Publishers Weekly

"THIS WHOLE NOVEL IS RIDICULOUS, OCCA-SIONALLY BAWDY AND MOST OF THE TIME LIGHT AS A BUBBLE—JUST AS IT SHOULD BE."

People magazine

MONSIEUR PAMPLEMOUSSE

Michael Bond

FAWCETT CREST • NEW YORK

Library of Congress Catalog Card Number: 84-24444

ISBN 0-449-20956-3

This edition published by arrangement with Beaufort Books, Inc.

Manufactured in the United States of America

First Ballantine Books Edition: March 1986

1

MONDAY EVENING

MONSIEUR PAMPLEMOUSSE DIPPED A LITTLE finger surreptitiously into the remains of some *sauce Madère* which had accompanied his *Filet de Boeuf en Croûte* and licked it reflectively before making a note on a small pad concealed beneath a flap in his right trouser leg.

Repeating the first part of the operation, he held his hand momentarily below the level of the table-cloth and felt the familiar roughness of a warm and appreciative tongue reach up to lick it clean.

A moment later there was a gentle stirring, followed by the padding of four large feet as Pommes Frites rose into view and made his way slowly across the floor of the restaurant.

A loud lapping sound coming from the direction of a water bowl situated just inside the entrance doors confirmed Monsieur Pamplemousse's worst suspicions. He underlined the note he had just made and then returned the pen to an inside pocket.

If Pommes Frites agreed that the *sauce Madère* was too salty, then too salty it was.

Strange that it should be so in such a renowned establishment as the Hôtel-Restaurant La Langoustine. In all the years he had been visiting St. Castille such a thing had never happened before. It could mean only one of two things; either an inexperienced and over-generous hand had been at the salt cellar in the kitchen—which seemed unlikely—or Auguste Douard, the chef-patron, was 'taking precautions'.

Putting salt in the Madeira to prevent staff from imbibing too much on the sly was an old trick, but in this case, with La Langoustine already the proud possessor of two Red Stock Pots in *Le Guide*, and well on its way to the supreme accolade of a third, such a move seemed not only unwarranted but positively foolhardy. Unless . . . Monsieur Pamplemousse resolved to keep a watchful eye on the situation. Over-indulgence of liquor was a recognised occupational hazard in the culinary world, but it was a hazard which needed to be resisted at all costs if one wished to scale the heights of the profession. It would be a disaster of the first magnitude if Monsieur Douard himself were to succumb to the bottle at this stage in his career.

Nevertheless, one had to be firm. There were standards which, once set, had to be maintained and lived up to. Working for *Le Guide* had taught him one thing: never to relax, never to take things for granted, always to savour, to analyse and compare.

The fillet of beef had been admirable; tender and lightly cooked beforehand to ensure that its juices were properly sealed within before being encased in its envelope of flaky pastry. As for the pastry, as ever it had been a miracle of lightness; the two together had made a magnificent, a heavenly combination. A slightly reckless choice for a first course, especially in view of what was to follow, but the journey had been a long one and there were two mouths to feed. Besides, it had been a very small portion—just enough to taste and report on. As things turned out he was glad he'd chosen it, for the accompanying sauce had definitely been below par.

Having justified the matter in his mind, Monsieur Pamplemousse helped himself to a solitary olive, mentally deducting another point from the restaurant's total for having failed to remove the plate when the first course arrived, and a further point from his own personal tally for being so weak.

Choosing a moment when all the waiters had their backs to him, he poured a quick glass of wine from a bottle cradled in a large, carved wooden sabot standing nearby, then he slipped the cork under the table for Pommes Frites to examine.

An approving sniff came from somewhere below the folds of the cloth. Given the choice, Pommes Frites much preferred Bordeaux, but he was no mean judge of Burgundy either. If it were possible to translate a sniff into oenological terms, then Pommes Frites' verdict was: 'If you *must* have a Côtes du Rhône instead of a decent Pauillac—and seeing we are more or less in the area, why not? —then what better than a '73 Hermitage?'

Monsieur Pamplemousse swirled the deep red liquid around in the glass, held it to his nose and sipped. The bouquet was superb, the taste complex and full of character. The vineyard must have

3

escaped the late hail storms of that year. It promised well.

Pushing aside the sabot, he tucked his napkin firmly inside his shirt collar in preparation for the next course, then turned his attention to his surroundings, reflecting as he did so that only in his beloved France could a restaurant combine all that was best in food with the worst excesses of interior design.

La Langoustine had reached its present eminence largely on account of its food. That, and an attention to detail in the hotel itself which was beyond reproach. The freshly cut flowers and the confiseries placed in all the rooms to welcome the guests when they arrived, the bowl of fruit beside every bed and the assortment of soaps and perfumes and after-shave lotions in the bathrooms, more than made up for any deficiencies in the décor.

But having said that, it had to be admitted that in other respects the hotel was a veritable monument to bad taste. Bad taste which had its roots in the days when wood was as plentiful and easy to come by as plastic is today.

Like her forbears, Madame Sophie Douard was deeply into wood and she, too, had added to the general effect in no mean way. Apart from the sabots and a large collection of old fire bellows which adorned the heavily panelled walls, wood in all its possible shapes and sizes and colours filled the dining room. But even these decorations were dwarfed by a trolley of positively heroic dimensions which occupied a position of honour in the centre of the room. Mounted on a pair of old cartwheels, it made the serving of sweets a hazard to both diner and waiter alike.

The Hôtel-Restaurant La Langoustine had stood in its present position for something like two hundred years. Founded by Madame Hortense Douard, who had won brief fame during the Revolution by delaying the approaching hordes by methods best left unreported, and whose memory was enshrined by a statue in the square outside, it had survived two world wars and between whiles prospered in its own quiet way.

When Auguste, fresh from catering college, met and married Sophie, he changed his name by deed poll so as to preserve the continuity of the Douard family. After a period of several years away from St. Castille, during which time he served his apprenticeship with some of the great names in French cuisine, he returned to take command following the death of Sophie's father, and from that day on La Langoustine had never looked back.

As Auguste's reputation spread far beyond boundaries never dreamed of by its founder, it began to cater for a more cosmopolitan clientele, and a further sign of the changing times lay in the fact that Madame Hortense's statue now boasted a fountain with twin jets which gushed forth from points neither nature nor its original creator had ever intended.

Lately, in anticipation of receiving his third Stock Pot, Auguste had taken to dropping his christian name in favour of plain Douard, and rumour had it that a cookery book—*Cuisine Douard*—was already in preparation, ready to be launched when the big moment arrived.

Work had lately begun on modernising the hotel—converting cupboards into extra toilets and box-rooms into en suite bathrooms, and plans were

5

under way for an extension to the building. Already cranes were poking their noses over the rooftop as a group of old outhouses at the rear was demolished to make way for the new.

Perhaps, by the time he came again, the postcard which he sent home as always, marking his room with its view of the garden, would be redundant. Monsieur Pamplemousse hoped not. He had the resistance to change which came with middle age.

The restaurant was beginning to fill up; a sprinkling of tourists—he was pleased to see an English couple deep in their copy of *Le Guide*, and at a table next to them two earnest American ladies, schoolteachers by their appearance, were busy working out where they had been on their gastronomic tour of Europe, and where they were going to next. For a moment he marvelled at the way such slender frames could emit such piercing voices and accommodate such vast quantities of food into the bargain. Perhaps the dissipation of all that energy in talk and travel enabled them to burn up the excess calories gained en route? Several tables were occupied by prosperous-looking businessmen, bemoaning the iniquities of governments past, present and future, and yet wearing their prosperity with accustomed ease; others by scientists from the nearby solar energy station. There was a courting couple who were paying more attention to each other than they were to the food. A young man at a crowded table in the middle of the room was making great play with his knowledge of wine—probably the son of a wealthy vigneron, for he spoke with authority.

And in the far corner, partly cut off from the rest

of the diners by a wooden screen, sat the blonde girl and her partner who had been responsible for the unpleasantness earlier in the evening.

Monsieur Pamplemousse stole a quick glance at her. Tall and slim, her clothes bore the unmistakable air of quality which only the very wealthy as opposed to the merely well-off can afford.

It had all been over in a matter of moments, but it had left a nasty taste in his Kir Royale. Certainly there was no trace of forgiveness in her pale blue eyes as they momentarily met his and held them. Eyes that matched her too impeccable accent; utterly without warmth. She looked as if she wished him anywhere but where he was sitting. He was unmoved.

The visit to the Hôtel-Restaurant La Langoustine was, for Monsieur Pamplemousse, an annual event, a way of killing two birds with one stone. The combining of business with pleasure was normally frowned on by the powers that be at *Le Guide*. Strict and unbiassed anonymity was the rule. But Monsieur Pamplemousse had been visiting the hotel for many years, following the rise in its fortunes with a friendly eye and an appreciative stomach, and each year he combined a brief holiday with an up-to-date report. Others would have to follow on, of course, to confirm his findings, particularly now it was in line for a further Stock Pot. That would mean a visit or two from Monsieur le Directeur himself. But his annual stay there was acknowledged to be sacrosanct.

He always occupied the same room, on the first floor at the back of the hotel, overlooking the garden and away from the noise of traffic in the main square.

Pommes Frites had a space reserved for his inflatable kennel below the window—not a bone's throw away from the kitchens, where he had many friends. Above all, they had their own special table in the restaurant. Monsieur Pamplemousse was a creature of habit; he needed certain parameters to which he could relate on his travels. It was the only way one could do the job and retain a degree of sanity and a healthy digestion.

He liked his table in the corner. From it he could watch the goings on in the rest of the room and yet remain relatively unnoticed. He could observe the arrival and departure of the other guests and keep a watchful eye on the staff as they bustled to and fro between kitchen and dining room. Above all, he was close enough to the entrance to overhear snatches of conversation when people left; little titbits which were invaluable when it came to making out his report.

All the more reason then, to feel deeply aggrieved when he came downstairs that evening and found the blonde girl engaged in a bitter argument with the maître d'hôtel on the subject of *his* table.

Normally accommodating in such matters, Monsieur Pamplemousse had politely but firmly stood his ground.

Fortunately Pommes Frites had taken the situation in at a glance and put an end to the discussion by settling himself down with such a proprietorial air it left no room for further argument.

All the same, it had been very disturbing while it lasted. The girl had taken it with particularly bad grace, and if the look she'd flung at Monsieur Pamplemousse as she and her companion were ushered to another table could have been translated into deeds, a certain part of his anatomy would by now have been sizzling merrily away in the sauté pan, destined for the doubtful privilege of appearing on the menu under the heading 'Dishes of the Day'.

Monsieur Pamplemousse shifted uneasily in his chair at the thought. And yet . . . despite, or perhaps because of her ill-temper, which had brought a becoming flush to her cheeks and a disconcerting rise and fall to her breasts, she had a certain fascination which he was not alone in appreciating. He'd noticed others in the room casting curious glances in the direction of the screen from time to time, obviously in the hope of catching another glimpse.

Monsieur Pamplemousse couldn't resist taking another quick look himself. As he did so he gave a start. Until that moment he'd hardly given the girl's companion more than a passing glance. He seemed a perfectly ordinary young man. Dark, possibly Italian from his looks; whereas he'd put the girl down as German or Scandinavian, her accent had been just a little too perfect. Discreetly dressed, obviously deeply embarrassed by the whole affair, he'd done his best to merge into the background, hardly uttering a word. Hands in his jacket pockets, he'd seemed only too anxious to escape behind the screen. Now Monsieur Pamplemousse could see why.

As he watched, the young man reached across the table to hand a dish to the girl. Almost immediately there was a crack like a pistol shot and it broke in two. The reason was simple. In place of a normal hand he had what looked like a steel claw, not unlike the grab on one of the mechanical excavators outside.

But there was worse to come. Brushing aside a waiter who rushed to his aid, the young man reached up with his other hand and revealed a second claw, identical to the first. Monsieur Pamplemousse drew in his breath with an involuntary gasp. Poor devil. What possible disaster could have been responsible for such a dreadful misfortune?

To his surprise the girl hardly seemed to notice, let alone offer to help. Instead, she had her eyes firmly fixed on the door leading to the kitchen as it swung open and a waiter bearing a large silver dish covered by a matching silver top entered the room and headed towards Monsieur Pamplemousse, where he placed it reverentially on a serving table in front of him.

The maître d'hôtel hurried forward.

Monsieur Pamplemousse looked at him with concern, the couple in the corner forgotten for the moment. The man looked as white as a sheet.

'Is anything the matter, Felix?'

'No, Monsieur Pamplemousse ... that is to say ...' Casting an anxious glance towards the kitchen, he wiped a bead of sweat from his brow. Then, seemingly reassured, he spread his hands out in the gesture of one whose fate is not of their choosing; a mixture of fatalistic acceptance of things past and apology for other events to come.

Monsieur Pamplemousse resolved to ignore everything in favour of concentrating on the task in hand. Everyone had their problems and doubtless all would be revealed in due course. There were more important things to think about. Already he could feel a stirring at his feet as Pommes Frites' nose inched its way out to investigate the arrival of the pièce de résistance.

One of the specialities of La Langoustine, in fact it would be true to say *the* speciality, was *Poularde de Bresse en Vessie Royale*; a whole chicken from Bresse, the best in all France, specially reared for Monsieur Douard and marked with his personal number by a private breeder, corn fed to precise instructions from the moment it was hatched to the day on which it was ready for the table, at which point it was carefully prepared with slices of truffle slipped beneath the skin and stuffed with seasoned foie gras. Placed inside a freshly scraped pig's bladder, which had been cleaned with salt and vinegar, it was then sewn up and cooked in a pot of chicken consommé for two and a half hours.

A dish fit for a king. Indeed, Auguste Douard had first prepared it for a minor royal personage who had chanced on the hotel, and it had remained on the menu ever since.

'*Voilà*, Monsieur!' Felix removed the domed lid with a flourish and then stood back mopping his brow again.

Monsieur Pamplemousse felt his mouth begin to water as the smell reached his nostrils. Pommes Frites gave a snuffle of anticipation, knowing full well that even his master couldn't tackle the whole of a dish which was normally meant for two.

The maître d'hôtel picked up a carving knife and a fork and stood with them poised, one in each hand. For some reason or other he seemed to have a strange reluctance to cut open the envelope where it had been sewn together. First he put the knife down, then he picked it up again, and each time he did so he gave a little moan.

Finally, unable to contain himself a moment longer, Monsieur Pamplemousse jumped to his feet.

'I do not know what has come over this restaurant tonight,' he exclaimed. 'Nor, at this stage, do I greatly care. Allow me. It is not going to bite you. At least, I sincerely hope not.'

For some reason his words had a devastating effect on Felix and his voice when it came was a barely audible croak. 'As you wish, Monsieur.' He backed away and clutched at the sweet trolley for support.

With the assurance of one who has seen it done a thousand times before, Monsieur Pamplemousse took the implements and with one deft movement pierced the bladder along its seam with the carving knife, at the same time pulling the gap apart with the fork. Then he stood back to admire his handiwork as the balloon-like outer casing collapsed on to the dish, revealing the contents for all to see.

As he did so the blood drained from his face. For a brief moment there was silence and then a woman screamed.

Monsieur Pamplemousse took a quick look round the room, noted in passing that the couple behind the screen were nowhere to be seen, then he sat down and gazed at the dish in front of him.

To say that the head looked vaguely familiar would have been a gross exaggeration in the circumstances. It was too misshapen to be readily identifiable as anything other than that of a man, perhaps, to judge by the matted covering of black hair, in his early thirties . . . and yet . . .

As if to sum up the feelings of all those present in the room, Pommes Frites lifted up his head and gave vent to a loud howl.

'Please,' said Monsieur Pamplemousse wearily

as the sound died away, 'will someone cover up this monstrosity before I make a similar noise.'

And then, instincts born out of years spent in not totally dissimilar situations coming to the fore, he stood up again and raised his hand for silence.

'I must ask that you all remain where you are for the time being. No one is to move until the police arrive.'

'I protest!' A man at a nearby table jumped to his feet and glared at him. 'My wife is upset. I demand to be allowed to leave. By what right . . .'

Monsieur Pamplemousse decided to take a chance. Reaching into an inside pocket he withdrew a small wallet, flicked it open, and flashed a card briefly through the air. 'By this right, Monsieur. And when I say no one,' he continued, 'that is precisely what I mean. No one.'

Monsieur Pamplemousse spoke with an air of quiet authority. An authority which many people over the years had good cause to remember, often to their cost. As he flicked the wallet shut and returned it to his pocket a faint smile crossed his face. Really, it was quite like old times.

'You realise that impersonating a police officer is an offence?'

'Impersonating?' Monsieur Pamplemousse raised his eyebrows in mock protest. 'Not for one single instant did I say I was a police officer. I merely showed them my American Express card. If they chose to . . .'

Inspector Banyuls brushed aside the words. His point had been made; his authority established. Leaning back in his chair he examined his fingernails. It was a meeting of opposites. The dislike had been mutual and instantaneous.

'I accept that you acted in what you considered to be the best interests. Nevertheless . . .' he looked up with a gesture which indicated that from now on, he, Inspector Banyuls, was in charge.

'Who would you consider most likely to wish to do you some harm?' The implication that the list could be a long one was not lost on Monsieur Pamplemousse.

'I have been retired from the Sûreté for several years now,' he began.

'Ah, yes . . .' Inspector Banyuls couldn't resist the opportunity. 'I remember now. It was in all the papers at the time. What was it they called it? The Case of the Cuckolded Chorus? Almost the whole of the line. How many girls were involved? Twenty-two?'

'Fifteen,' growled Monsieur Pamplemousse. 'It was a trumped-up charge. Besides, anyone who wanted to do me harm would have done so long ago.'

'Some husbands have long memories . . . As for lovers . . .'

'Were I still in Paris, perhaps . . . but in this part of the world?'

'It has all the marks of the Mafia. A warning perhaps? Keep off . . . next time . . .' Inspector Banyuls made the classic throat-cutting gesture. Despite himself, Monsieur Pamplemousse couldn't help but feel a shiver run down his spine. Banyuls was right.

'These things . . . the Mafia, they are more of the South than of the North.'

'Nevertheless, you say you recognised the head?'

'It looked familiar, that is all.'

Inspector Banyuls tried a different approach. 'Why are you here?'

'It is a private matter. One that need not concern you.' Monsieur Pamplemousse returned the other's gaze without blinking.

'And you are leaving, when?'

'I have yet to decide. It depends.'

'Depends?'

Monsieur Pamplemousse refused to be drawn. Instead he cupped his hands round a large balloon-shaped glass to warm it and then sniffed the contents with an air of well-being.

'Would you care to join me in an Armagnac? It is the '28. A great year. I can recommend it. It is the patron's Réserve d'Artagnan. A whiff of Three Musketeers country. One can taste the oak from the forest of Monzelun.' Even as he spoke he knew he was saying the wrong thing.

'I wouldn't know, Pamplemousse. The pay of an inspector in the French police does not allow for such pleasures—even before retirement. One day you must let me know how you manage it. And now . . .' he rose, 'there is work to be done. There are others to be questioned. I must thank you again for your foresight in retaining them. Perhaps some will have a better memory of the event than you appear to.'

Monsieur Pamplemousse acknowledged the words with a nod. He'd been about to remark on the absence of the young couple, but he decided against it. Why should he put himself out? The problem was Inspector Banyuls' concern, not his. Had he been Inspector Banyuls there were a number of questions which would have required an answer.

Where, for example, was Madame Douard?

In all the years he'd been visiting La Langoustine she had never been absent from her post, greeting guests as they arrived, visiting all the tables to make sure everyone was happy. He hadn't seen her all the evening. It was very odd.

Monsieur Douard was also conspicuous by his absence. Busy though he always was, he was never too busy to pop out for a quick greeting. Tonight he was nowhere to be seen.

Then there was the extraordinary behaviour of Felix.

Last, but not least, there was the matter of the head.

Lifelike though it undoubtedly was—or had been before the application of heat—the inescapable fact remained that it was made of plastic, pinkish brown, shiny plastic, something he'd realised straight away on closer inspection.

Alors! He turned his attention to the Armagnac. 1928. The year of his birth. Was that why he had chosen it? Or was it some perverse and rather petty desire to score over the inspector; to show that although he might be retired he certainly wasn't yet out of the running? If so, it was an unworthy motive—one which would have disappointed the makers had they been present. Such ambrosial spirit was meant for higher things.

It was also meant to be savoured in peace and quiet. Really, the noise in the restaurant had reached an intolerable level. Even Inspector Banyuls seemed to have lost something of his cool as he did battle with the rest of the occupants, each trying to get a word in first.

Watching him run a distraught hand round the

inside of his shirt collar, Monsieur Pamplemousse felt a pang of sympathy. Perhaps, despite his dislike of the other, he should have been more co-operative. Fuelled by the warmth of the liquid now at work in his veins, his feeling of remorse grew. He felt a sudden desire to mount a rescue operation; to create a diversion. A wicked gleam came into his eyes.

Rapping his empty glass sharply on the table, he stood up and cleared his throat. Almost immediately the room fell silent.

'Everyone,' he said, choosing his words with care, 'seems most concerned about the *Poularde de Bresse en Vessie Royale*—or perhaps in the circumstances I should say the *Tête en Vessie Royale*—with which I was served earlier in the evening, but which, I hasten to add, I did not touch. Not a morsel passed my lips. But no one yet seems to have considered the fact that the head of this unfortunate young man was once attached to a body and that a body has many parts.'

Here Monsieur Pamplemousse paused for effect, conscious that all eyes were on him.

He turned to a woman nearby. 'I notice, Madame, that you ordered the *Pâté de Cervelle en Croûte*—brains in pastry. I trust they were to your liking? Not too smooth?

'And you, Monsieur, did you enjoy your liver? Or do you now wish you'd ordered the *truite*?

'As for you, Monsieur, I believe you had the hearts?'

Pressing home his advantage remorselessly, Monsieur Pamplemousse looked towards the American ladies. 'I couldn't help overhearing you ask for your leg of lamb to be well done. A wise decision.

If it had been too rare it might have acquired even more of a nightmarish quality in the years to come.'

He glanced down at the menu. 'I see they have *andouillette*. Now, that would have been quite an experience . . .'

Monsieur Pamplemousse was enjoying himself. Now that he was beginning to warm to his theme there were all sorts of exciting possibilities.

But his pleasure was short-lived. The silence which followed his remarks was broken by a loud crunching sound. It came from a spot somewhere near his feet.

'*Sapristi!*' Monsieur Pamplemousse turned and gazed at the empty dish on his serving table. 'Oh, my word! Oh, my very word!'

Pommes Frites gazed unhappily around the room, a rivulet of pinkish gravy running down his chin. He liked an audience and one way and another he'd been feeling pretty left out of things. Not only that, but he'd been getting more and more hungry. Now, both situations had been well and truly rectified; the former in a way which left little to be desired, the latter in a way which left a great deal. Never in the whole of his life had he tasted anything quite so disgusting.

On the other side of the room someone was noisily sick.

Monsieur Pamplemousse was pleased to see it was Inspector Banyuls. At least when Pommes Frites disgraced himself he gave value for money.

2

TUESDAY MORNING

POMMES FRITES WAS FED UP. FED UP AND IN disgrace; or fed up because he was in disgrace. It amounted to much the same thing in the end. Everywhere he went in St. Castille he left a trail of 'Oooh, la la!'s, as passers-by pointed him out and recounted their version of the previous night's escapade.

And as he continued his perambulations so the story was repeated and handed on, growing in horror and complexity, until by the time he got back to the Square du Centre mothers were running out into the street to grab their protesting children and drag them indoors lest his appetite and taste for blood got the better of him again.

Convicted on circumstantial evidence, that's what he'd been.

Inspector Banyuls had not been pleased. If Inspector Banyuls had had his way, banishment to an open-ended kennel in Siberia during the depths of winter would have been among the least of his punishments. There had been talk of arrest and charges of consuming vital evidence with criminal intent.

Just because he'd happened to be standing near the empty dish at the time and happened to have gravy on his chin. It wouldn't have been quite so bad if he'd enjoyed his meal, but he couldn't remember ever having eaten anything quite so unappetising before; he could still taste it. If he, Pommes Frites, had any say in the matter not only would La Langoustine be out of the running for a further Stock Pot, they would lose the two they already possessed.

Unkindest cut of all, in all the excitement he'd been sent to bed supperless. It was a good job he'd remembered a small cache of bones buried in the garden during a previous visit, otherwise he might have starved to death. Then they would have been sorry. It was not quite what his taste buds had been expecting, but in the circumstances better than nothing.

Even his master's defence of his actions had seemed a little half-hearted. But at least he had tried, bringing to bear such arguments as he could muster to make the point that Pommes Frites couldn't be blamed for giving way to what were, after all, only his animal instincts.

Animal instincts indeed! In his time Pommes Frites had dined at some of the best restaurants in France, and although he wouldn't, and most certainly didn't, ever turn up his nose at the odd biscuit or two when they were offered, there were limits.

To show the extent of his displeasure he left his

mark against the side of the fountain and then confirmed everyone's worst suspicions by baring his teeth at a small boy who had come to watch, adding a rather satisfactory growling noise for good measure.

As the child ran off screaming, Pommes Frites began to feel slightly better. He made his way across the square towards the hotel and peered in at the bar in the hope that his master might have finished breakfast and be ready to join him in another stroll.

But Monsieur Pamplemousse was deep in conversation with the patron. In fact, had the question been put to him in so many words, a walk was not high on Monsieur Pamplemousse's agenda at that moment in time. He had other things to think about. One way and another he'd spent a sleepless night and while listening to Monsieur Douard he was fortifying himself with an early morning *marc* over his coffee, strictly for medicinal purposes, of course. It was the least he could do for his nerves.

Pommes Frites hesitated, torn between the thought of another stroll and not wanting to miss anything. In the end curiosity won the day and he curled up comfortably at his master's feet, pretending he was asleep but in reality keeping a weather eye open for possible clues which might help him to redeem his lost reputation.

'Such a thing has never happened before!' Monsieur Douard, his head buried in his hands, was going back over things for the umpteenth time.

'Always I am down in the kitchen in good time for the evening's work, while Sophie gets ready to welcome the guests . . . and yet, last night . . . I do not know what came over us. One moment we were awake, I in my room, Sophie in hers, the next moment ... poof! ... we were out like a light. No one could awaken us. Thank heaven for Pierre.

'Pierre is my new chef de cuisine. He trained in much the same way as I did—at the same school, in fact. Mark my words, a spell with Bocuse, or perhaps the Troisgros brothers, and one day he, too, will have his own restaurant. Perhaps he will be the first to win three Stock Pots in his native Brittany. The kitchen of a restaurant is like the bridge of an ocean liner—it can, and often does, function without its captain. Nevertheless, things are not quite the same. Pierre is good, and in time he will be even better, but he has been brought up by the sea—he has it in his blood. I tell him, sometimes he is a little too fond of the salt. He is also lacking in fire. If I had been in my kitchen last night those *maquereaux* would not have got away with it as they did.'

Monsieur Pamplemousse breathed a sigh of relief. He decided to try one more test.

'Will you join me in a *marc*?'

Monsieur Douard raised his hands in mock horror. 'I have a busy day ahead of me. Later, perhaps, but if I were to start now ...'

Things were beginning to fall into place. The absence of Madame Douard at dinner. The non-appearance of Auguste. The general air of things not being quite as they should have been. The over-salted *sauce Madère* ... only one more item remained unexplained. No doubt Inspector Banyuls had already posed the question, but there would be no harm in asking it again.

'I still don't understand how the change round of dishes came about. It couldn't have been easy.'

Auguste Douard made a clucking noise. 'Ah, poor Felix. I fear we shall not be seeing him before tonight. He has taken to his bed. He was attacked in the pantry earlier in the afternoon by an armed assailant—disguised, would you believe, as a waiter?'

Monsieur Pamplemousse felt that by now he would believe almost anything.

'While the kitchen was empty,' continued Auguste dramatically, 'this same man forced him at gun point and under threat of death, to substitute a dish he had brought with him for the real one. As you know, *Poularde de Bresse en Vessie Royale* has to be ordered in advance.'

'And how many were ordered last night?'

'Five others besides your own. I supervised their preparation earlier in the day.'

Monsieur Pamplemousse fell silent. So the one which had arrived at his table had not necessarily been meant for him.

'I have a theory.' Monsieur Douard forestalled his next question. 'It is my belief that someone wishes to bring disgrace on the house of Douard. As you will understand, I have many rivals, some of whom would stick at nothing.'

'Isn't that a bit extreme?'

'Extreme?' Auguste Douard dismissed the thought. 'You have no idea of the rivalry, no idea. Especially,' he cast a sidelong glance at Monsieur Pamplemousse, 'especially when it is an open secret that La Langoustine is in the running for a third Stock Pot.

'There is big money involved. To have three Stock Pots in *Le Guide,* or three stars in Michelin,

23

or even four toques in Gault Millau, is an open-sesame to other things; a pass-key to many doors which would otherwise remain closed. One reaches another plateau. Have you ever been in a restaurant on the day they receive news of their third Stock Pot? The telephone doesn't stop ringing. There are offers for lecture tours, television programmes, books ... merchandising rights ... many men would give their right arm for such opportunities, and equally many would stop at nothing to prevent others reaching that goal. As in all fields, success brings its problems. For every person who reaches the heights there are others waiting in the wings. Alors ...'

Monsieur Pamplemousse gave him an oblique glance. Auguste Douard clearly wished to say something, but equally clearly he was unsure whether it was safe to or not.

He decided to test the water. 'You have something on your mind, Monsieur?'

Auguste took a deep breath. 'You are a man of the world, Monsieur Pamplemousse, accustomed to eating in the best restaurants, staying at the best hotels, drinking the best wines ...

'Suppose ... suppose, for example, you had been in the position last night of having to pass judgment on La Langoustine? A judgment that might well affect its entire future. How would you be feeling this morning in the cold light of day?'

Monsieur Pamplemousse busied himself with his coffee. So his secret was out. *Merde!* What would they say back at headquarters if they knew? It would be a black mark. Monsieur le Directeur would not be pleased.

Auguste Douard read his thoughts. 'You must

understand that any man who dines regularly by himself and orders with an air of authority is an object of interest, particularly at this time of the year when all the guides are being prepared. The man from Michelin we usually recognise because he is for ever drawing little symbols in his diary and going through the menu to make sure there are no spelling mistakes—they are very meticulous, those ones. The man from Gault Millau, on the other hand, is much more concerned with his nouvelle cuisine and after he has left we find many notes torn up in the waste bucket. They are very fond of their purple prose. Those from the English guides ask "What is for breakfast?" Whereas . . .'

'Whereas?' Monsieur Pamplemousse prodded him gently.

Auguste Douard looked round carefully to make sure they were alone before replying.

'Monsieur Pamplemousse, you are an honoured and most welcome guest in our hotel. You and Pommes Frites. It has always been that way and I trust it will remain so in the future. Your reputation in the Sûreté as a man who never gave up on a case, often and sadly to his cost, has gone before you. Your taste in food and in wine is something I have observed with pleasure over the years, and your approval is a reward in itself. I ask for nothing more. In matters of cuisine I am content to be judged by what is set before you. In the end there is no other way. Your secret is safe with me.

'But I will not conceal from you the fact that last night's affair came as a great shock, not simply because of its nature, but because of its timing. As you know, we have many plans for the hotel; many commitments. We have much at stake.

'To win the approval of Michelin is a great honour; to gain a further toque in Gault Millau, that, too, would be good. But to receive a third Stock Pot in *Le Guide*—the oldest, the most respected in all France, that would mean so much I cannot possibly put it into words. I repeat, I ask no favours as far as your judgment on the food is concerned. I would not insult either you or *Le Guide* by suggesting such a thing. However, if there is some way in which you can help to solve this mystery I shall be more than grateful.'

Monsieur Pamplemousse considered the matter for a moment or two, conscious that the other was watching his every movement.

'Were what you have just said about me true,' he hedged, 'it would have been even more unfortunate if I had recommended last night's dish as a speciality. Think what that might involve in the future.' He chuckled at the thought and then immediately repented. Monsieur Douard was obviously in no mood for such frivolities.

'Rest assured, Auguste,' he placed one hand on the other's arm and allowed himself the luxury of familiarity, 'if it is within my power to help in any way during my stay here, then I shall be happy to do so. I must confess my curiosity has already been aroused. As for the other matter, if I were in a position to pass judgment then in no way would I allow what happened to influence my decision.'

He clasped the other's hand warmly in his own and then rose from the table. For some reason or other Pommes Frites had become increasingly agitated, and glancing out through the door he could see why. The young man with the artificial hands was crossing the square. He was by himself and he seemed in a hurry. His companion—the girl—aloof as ever, was heading towards the main part of the town carrying a shopping bag. Gucci by the look of it.

'Thank you, my friend.' Auguste waved as Monsieur Pamplemousse made his way outside. 'I feel better already. A man should not enter his kitchen in a mood of despair. He should be in a state of grace. Tonight I shall prepare something very special indeed—just for you!'

But Monsieur Pamplemousse scarcely heard. His mind was already on other things. Crossing the square, he was just in time to see steel-claws, as he'd mentally christened the young man, round a corner near the P.T.T. and disappear up a side street.

Signalling Pommes Frites to heel, he waited for a moment or two and then hurried after him.

Like many towns in the region, St. Castille had been spared the outer sprawl of industrialisation. It began and ended abruptly, almost as if surrounded by an invisible moat. Once past the grey, gaunt building of the hospice which marked the boundary they were in open country.

Hardly slackening speed, the young man began the steady climb up a narrow road leading towards the plateau which lay at the foot of the hills and mountains to the east.

Once, early on, a car shot past, scattering Monsieur Pamplemousse and Pommes Frites as it took a bend ahead at high speed.

Breathing heavily as he jumped down from the boulder which had acted as a temporary refuge, Monsieur Pamplemousse shook his fist after both car and driver as they disappeared up the hill in a cloud of dust. Whoever was at the wheel might know the road, but he was no respecter of persons.

Beyond the treeline some miles ahead he could see a cluster of buildings which he guessed must be the new solar heating station, St. Castille's contribution to the march of progress. No doubt they were deriving pleasure and profit from the warmth of the day—which was more than he could say. Even Pommes Frites was beginning to flag a little and he hung back for a moment to slake his thirst noisily from a brook, babbling its way down the hill. Some bees from a nearby cluster of hives buzzed their disapproval at the intrusion and then settled down again.

Monsieur Pamplemousse mopped his brow while he waited. It was pointless indulging in any sort of cat and mouse game. Apart from a few olive trees and the odd clump of gorse, the countryside ahead offered little or no cover.

A lizard appeared as if by magic on a nearby stone, froze, and then carried on its way. Overhead a bird hovered for a moment and then it, too, went on its way.

Throwing caution to the wind, he quickened his pace as they set off again. He had no wish to turn the whole thing into a cross-country race, but if he didn't catch up by the time they reached flatter ground that was what might happen.

But the young man seemed to be displaying no interest whatsoever in his surroundings. Hands thrust deep into his pockets, just as they had been in the restaurant the night before, he went on his way—looking neither to the right nor to the left. And yet Monsieur Pamplemousse was left with the curious feeling that not only did he know he was being followed, but he actually wanted it.

Already the terracotta rooftops of St. Castille were far below, lost in the morning heat haze. Apart from a few sheep and the solitary figure of a man with a shotgun slung over his shoulder on a rise to the right of them—doubtless a farmer trying to fill the evening cooking pot—they could have been alone in the world.

In other circumstances Monsieur Pamplemousse might have enjoyed it more. As it was he was beginning to wish himself back in Paris. The sheer scale of it all; the grandeur of the distant Alps outlined against the perfect blueness of the sky, the hum of the insects, the smell of the wildflowers, were lost on him. Head down, he found himself wondering what had ever possessed anyone to build such a road in the first place. Where on earth had they been going and for what purpose? Come to that, what was he doing there? What would his colleagues at headquarters think if they could see him now? He'd really only set off on a whim. For a second or two he toyed with the idea of turning back. It was all rather ridiculous.

Occupied as he was with these thoughts, he failed to notice his quarry had stopped until he was almost on top of him. By then it was too late to do anything about it.

'Will you please stop following me?' Steel-claws sounded over-wrought. 'I know what you're going to say.'

Monsieur Pamplemousse took out a handkerchief, already wet with perspiration, and mopped his brow again while he played for time. He was momentarily at a loss for words. To be truthful he hadn't the least idea what he'd been going to say.

'You were going to ask about these, weren't you?' The young man held up both hands. They glinted in the sunshine.

'What about them?' If that was what he wanted it was as good an opening conversational gambit as any.

'I knew it! I knew it! You're all the same. Why can't you leave me alone?'

Monsieur Pamplemousse felt somewhat aggrieved. To give him his due, although the matter of the mechanical hands was not without interest, they hadn't been uppermost in his mind. He certainly wouldn't normally have been so unfeeling as to pose a direct question on the subject without being prompted.

'You don't *have* to tell me.'

'You're not going to believe me if I do. No one ever does.'

'You could try me if you wish,' said Monsieur Pamplemousse gently.

The young man sat down on a stone at the side of the road and gazed out across the valley. 'I used to work for a large catering firm,' he began at last. 'Grimaldi. You may have heard of them. Refrigerators ... deep freezes ... kitchen equipment ... that sort of thing. Waste disposals ...'

Monsieur Pamplemousse caught his breath. 'You don't mean ...'

The young man nodded miserably. 'The trouble is I've never been very good with my hands.' He broke off. 'That's a laugh as things turned out.

'Some people are mechanically-minded, some aren't—never will be. I was demonstrating our latest model—the Mark IV industrial size with the last-for-life bearings and the optional U-train recycling attachment, when something went wrong. I should by rights have sent for a mechanic, but it could have been a big order so I tried to fix it myself and that's when it happened. I put my hand down inside and whoosh! There it was—gone!'

They fell silent as Monsieur Pamplemousse tried to picture the scene.

'It must have been a very big machine,' he ventured at last. 'I mean . . . to accommodate two.'

His companion gave a shrill laugh. 'That's what's so ridiculous. That's the bit you're really not going to believe.'

'You mean . . .' Monsieur Pamplemousse shuddered at the thought. 'You didn't do it a *second* time?'

'There was a big investigation, you see . . . afterwards. All the pezzi-grossi from Rome were there. They asked me to show them exactly what went wrong, so I put my other hand inside and . . . and . . .'

Monsieur Pamplemousse gazed at the young man. He was glad he'd been spared the second 'whoosh'. To paraphrase that great Irish writer, Oscar Wilde, losing one hand was a misfortune, losing two in the same manner was downright careless.

'You've no idea, *no idea* what it's like . . .'

Monsieur Pamplemousse shifted uneasily. He realised he had been standing perfectly still for some minutes, hanging on the other's every word. That, combined with the long, uphill walk, had brought on a certain stiffness; his shins felt quite painful. What could he say? What words could he possibly find to meet the young man on common ground? What personal misfortune could he conjure up to even begin to match the other's?

He was a kindly man at heart and as he pondered the matter an outrageous thought entered his mind; one which had he dwelt on it for any length of time he would have dismissed out of hand. As it was, almost without thinking and with the highest possible motives, he found himself giving voice to an untruth.

'Monsieur,' he said simply, 'I do not know your name, but fate seems to have thrown us together for a short while and I have to tell you that you are not alone. You do not have a monopoly on misfortune.'

The young man stared at him. 'What are you trying to tell me?'

Monsieur Pamplemousse tapped the secret compartment in his right trouser leg, the one containing his precious note-book. It gave out a hollow, wooden sound.

'Does that sound like flesh and blood to you?'

'You don't mean . . . it isn't?'

Monsieur Pamplemousse nodded. Then, having embarked on a certain course, decided that he might as well be hanged for a sheep as a lamb.

'And that is not all.'

'Not . . . both?'

Monsieur Pamplemousse nodded again. Conscious that Pommes Frites' eyes were following his every movement, he avoided the direct lie. It was totally idiotic, but there it was. There was no going back.

'That's terrible. I'm sorry. I would never have known.' It was the young man's turn to be tongue-tied. For one moment Monsieur Pamplemousse thought he was going to cry.

'By the way, it's Giampiero.'

'Giampiero?'

'My name.' The young man thrust out his right hand for Monsieur Pamplemousse to shake and then withdrew it hastily. 'I'm sorry. I'm always doing that. I still haven't got used to it.'

For some strange reason Monsieur Pamplemousse found himself registering the fact that before his accident Giampiero must have had very long arms; almost apelike. Perhaps that was what had brought it about. Perhaps if they had been two or three inches shorter it wouldn't have happened.

'Fancy having *two* wooden legs. I don't know what to say.'

'Poof!' Monsieur Pamplemousse waved his own hand carelessly in the air. Then, as he caught sight of it, immediately felt guilty.

There was an embarrassed silence. 'That is life,' he continued. 'Don't ask me how it happened. Like you, I would really rather not talk about it. Besides, it all took place long ago. I merely wished to show that however bad things may seem, there is always someone a little worse off. No one is entirely without their private sorrows.'

He broke off. Out of the corner of his eye he could see Pommes Frites stalking off towards a large gorse bush by the side of the road. On its own, not an unusual occurrence. What distinguished this particular occasion from previous ones was the fact that he would have sworn on oath the bush in question hadn't been there when they had first arrived. It was most odd. Perhaps he had been standing out in the sun for too long, or maybe he'd over-indulged himself with the *marc* at breakfast. Auguste was right; one should take care. Nevertheless ... Monsieur Pamplemousse dismissed the matter from his mind, putting it down as a momentary aberration; a summing-up which would have echoed Pommes Frites' feelings almost exactly had he been able to put them into words. Such things did not happen.

Even so, as he investigated the bush Pommes Frites couldn't help feeling a certain amount of surprise that it smelled strongly of bay rum instead of gorse. Just as he was in the very act of raising his right leg his attention was caught by something else strange. The bush was beginning to rotate very slowly on its axis in a clock-wise direction. Pommes Frites gazed at it in astonishment for a moment and then hurried round the back in the same clock-wise manner in order to keep up with his chosen spot. He had a wide experience of bushes in all shapes and sizes, but he couldn't remember such a thing ever happening before.

As the bush settled down again he decided to have another go, devoting all his attention this time to the job in hand, lest it began playing any more tricks. Balancing on three legs while at the same time keeping a watchful eye open for possible attackers from the rear demands a certain amount of concentration. A moment's relaxation, especially if the bush happens to be of a thorny variety, can be very painful.

Pommes Frites concentrated, and as he did so he became aware of something else that was odd. It was a large bush and it wasn't planted in the ground as were most bushes he'd come across, it was being held by someone; someone moreover who appeared to be clutching a long, shiny object in his other hand. Only an inch or two away from the end of Pommes Frites' nose there was a large expanse of blue, pin-striped suiting. He blinked several times in order to make quite sure that he was seeing aright, but the object was definitely made of some kind of material. Material, moreover, that was stretched almost to bursting point by virtue of the fact that whoever was inside it was bending over.

Never one to let an opportunity slip by, Pommes Frites gave the material an exploratory sniff.

As sniffs go it wasn't one of his best efforts. In his time he'd done many better, but the effect left absolutely nothing to be desired.

To his astonishment the object of his attentions suddenly leapt into the air and went off bang—right in his face.

Without waiting to find out the cause of this extraordinary occurrence, let alone complete his *renverser la vapeur*, Pommes Frites took off like a sheet of greased lightning. He was vaguely aware of shouts and cries and the sound of a car being driven off at high speed, but by the time he peered out from his hiding place all was quiet again.

Assured that whatever had caused the phenomenon had gone on its way, he emerged and noticed for the first time that although his master was more or less where he'd last seen him, he was now lying on the ground with one leg in the air. Pommes Frites decided it was obviously one of 'those mornings', and he hurried across the road in order to take a closer look and see if he could find out exactly what had happened.

Monsieur Pamplemousse could have told him. Monsieur Pamplemousse could have told him in no uncertain terms what had taken place as seen from the other side of the bush. The whole thing was indelibly imprinted on his mind. Pommes Frites' view had been from the wings as it were—a peep behind the scenes; his role that of prompter. Monsieur Pamplemousse, on the other hand, had viewed it all from stage centre and had, when he thought back over the chain of events later that day, played the leading role, escaping death or at the very least being maimed for life by a matter of millimetres.

It had all happened in a flash, although at the time it seemed more like a bad dream taking place in slow motion. He'd been vaguely aware of seeing Pommes Frites amble off in the direction of the bush. He'd also felt there was something 'not quite right' when he'd seen him disappear round the back, but he'd been taken up with other matters. Then all at once the bush had taken off like a missile from its launch pad. There had been a flash of sunlight on metal, followed by a loud bang, and then something hit him in the right leg, knocking him off balance and causing him to fall to the ground.

Like Pommes Frites he'd also been aware of a figure running from the bush and the sound of an engine starting up, but by the time he'd recovered himself sufficiently to do anything about it the car was already almost out of sight and it was too late to catch its number.

He felt the top of his leg. The trousers were torn and peppered with small holes, but by some miracle which could only have been arranged by his own personal guardian angel—the one who had watched over him all the years he'd been in the force—the shot seemed to have been taken fairly and squarely by his note-book.

'Mamma Mia!' Giampiero returned from an abortive pursuit of the car. He seemed remarkably calm in the circumstances. More relieved than upset. 'That was a bit of luck!'

'Luck?' Monsieur Pamplemousse could hardly believe his ears.

'Well, I mean your having a wooden leg. Think what it would have been like otherwise. It could have been very nasty.'

Monsieur Pamplemousse clambered to his feet and dusted himself down. Not for the first time that morning he was finding difficulty in expressing himself.

'*Merde!*' he muttered under his breath. '*Idiot! Imbécile!*'

As he stomped off down the road he felt a pain in his leg, or rather a series of tiny pains rolled into one, rather as if someone had hit him with a wire brush. Some of the shot had obviously penetrated the skin. Who knew what vital organs they might have made contact with had they spread any further? Organs that might have required the surgeon's knife.

'There's a very good carpenter in the town,' called Giampiero. 'Madame Sophie will give you his name.'

But Monsieur Pamplemousse was already out of sight round a bend in the road and taking stock of the situation. Settling himself down behind an outcrop of rock he gazed sadly at the tattered remains of his notebook, his aide-mémoire, while Pommes Frites busied himself licking the wounds. What months of hard work, what meals they had consumed were recorded within its covers. Now it looked more like a kit of parts for a cardboard colander.

Someone, somewhere, was going to pay dearly for this. If he'd had any doubts before about the wisdom of staying on in St. Castille, they had now gone for ever.

Pommes Frites looked up from his ministrations and wagged his tail in anticipation. He knew the signs.

3

TUESDAY EVENING

AUGUSTE DOUARD REMOVED A LARGE EARTH-enware marmite from his oven, placed it on top of the 'piano' which ran the length of the kitchen, and gave the contents a stir with a long wooden spoon. Having tested the result to his satisfaction, he slid the pot further along towards the cooler end and then turned to Monsieur Pamplemousse.

'For you,' he said, 'I am preparing a *tian*. It is not a dish you will often find in restaurants. It belongs more to the home . . . it is a family dish. In some of the smaller villages up in the mountains it is still sent out to be cooked in the oven of the *boulanger*. It is a *gratin* of green vegetables; spinach, chard, courgettes—all finely chopped and then cooked in olive oil. After that, some rice, beans, a few cloves of garlic, some eggs to thicken and a coating of breadcrumbs and Parmesan cheese. Up here, away from the coast, we also add a little salt cod to taste or some wild asparagus when it is in season.'

He smacked his lips. 'I think you will enjoy it. It is a good, peasant dish and it will need a good, robust wine to accompany it. A Cornas from the Rhône valley would go well. I háve a friend there who has land on the steepest part of the slopes. It is sheltered from the Mistral and he makes wines of great power. He always keeps a little to one side for me. It needs to be ten years old at least.

'Afterwards, perhaps a Banon or a Bleu d'Auvergne. It is a good time of the year for it. The milk is from herds high up in the mountains and we know a very special farm where it is made. Unpasteurised . . . the best!'

Monsieur Pamplemousse found himself envying Auguste his circle of friends. It was really partly what it was all about: knowing the right places to buy. He glanced around the kitchen. He never ceased to be surprised by the quietness of it all. Far removed from the popular image, where it was all shouting and noise. In most big kitchens he'd been lucky enough to enter, only the chef himself had a right to speak and when he did everyone jumped to it.

He wondered idly if Monsieur Douard's choice of a dish which had to be cooked in a stockpot was intentional, a hint. Then he dismissed the thought as being uncharitable. Auguste Douard was one of nature's gentlemen; he would not be so devious. His next words confirmed the thought.

'My poor friend. All these years and until today I had no idea. From your walk no one would ever have guessed. Although I have to admit that now I do know I detect a slight limp.'

Once again Monsieur Pamplemousse found himself regretting the story he'd concocted on the spur of the moment. He'd done it with the best of intentions, but throwing out a crumb of comfort for Giampiero was one thing—deceiving others who trusted him was something else again. The only consolation was that the limp Auguste detected was very real. His leg was still smarting from the attentions of the local chemist.

But Auguste already had other things on his mind. Sensing that Monsieur Pamplemousse did not wish to discuss the matter he changed the subject rapidly.

'Oh, what a day it has been!' He ran his eye briefly over the clipboard to which the first of the evening's orders had already been attached, then briefly gave out a few orders with hardly a change of voice. 'First the examining magistrate poking about here, there and everywhere—trying to sound important, then Inspector Banyuls. And they all expect their little *pourboire*. As if they were doing *me* a service! How would they like it if I went into their offices and helped myself to the stationery? Just because I happen to run a restaurant they feel everything should be on the house. Honesty has strange boundaries, even with the law itself.

'Now they have decided to leave someone permanently on guard in case there is another incident. What a way to greet one's guests—an armed policeman in the hall!

'I sometimes think only a fool would go into this business. A fool, or someone who is born with eyes in the back of his head.' With a wave of his hand he embraced the whole of the kitchen. 'They are all good people—the best; but at the end of the day it is not their head which is on the chopping block, it is mine. Each and every day—twice a day—my work is offered up for examination and discussion and analysis. Unless I watch their every move and check this, taste that, add a little here, take away a little there, there will be a sauce which is too thick, or a steak which is overdone, or vegetables that have not been properly cleaned. How can I be expected to watch out for criminals in the pantry as well?'

Monsieur Pamplemousse excused himself. More orders were starting to arrive; the pace was quickening. It was no place to linger.

Pommes Frites was waiting for him in the hall, keeping a watchful eye on the gendarme. Pommes Frites and gendarmes didn't always see eye to eye. Together they made their way into the dining room where Felix was waiting to usher them to their table.

'A bad business, Monsieur. You are happy? You would not like to sit elsewhere?'

'Very happy, thank you.' He wasn't going to give up his table for anyone. Apart from anything else he welcomed the opportunity to take stock of the restaurant again.

It was less full than usual. News had obviously travelled fast. No doubt there were many who had been put off, at least for the time being. They would be back—it would be their loss if they didn't return. There would probably be fewer orders for the *Poularde en Vessie*. If Monsieur Douard had not prepared the *tian* he might have been tempted to order one out of sheer bravado.

One or two of the diners nudged each other as he sat down. Some stared quite openly. He noted that Giampiero was already seated with his girl friend, if that was what she was—he must check to see if she was wearing a ring—but there was no hint of recognition. He mentally shrugged his shoulders. If that was the way they wanted it, then so be it. They must have started their meal early, for they were already on the cheese course.

Felix came between him and his line of vision, flicked open a serviette, and with rather more ostentation than usual held it out for Monsieur Pamplemousse to take.

Once again he appeared to be behaving rather oddly. It crossed Monsieur Pamplemousse's mind to wonder if he was in for a repeat performance of the previous night's occurrence, but he dismissed it at once. Auguste was on duty in the kitchen. Besides, he'd seen him plunge the spoon deep into the *tian* with his own eyes. If there had been anything untoward inside it would undoubtedly have been revealed. All the same, he had to admit the thought was not a pleasant one.

What on earth was the man doing? Either give him the serviette or not. Each time he reached for it Felix danced away like a matador who has seen better days.

'A note, Monsieur Pamplemousse,' hissed Felix.

Monsieur Pamplemousse gave a start. Sure enough, partly concealed within the folds of the white serviette, and held in place by Felix's thumb, was a piece of lined paper.

'It is from the gentleman in the corner. The one with whom there was the unpleasantness last night. It is a matter of the utmost discretion.'

Monsieur Pamplemousse nodded. 'Leave it on the table. I will look at it in a moment.'

But he needn't have worried. There was no question of either Giampiero or his companion taking the slightest bit of notice. They were much too busy talking.

Monsieur Pamplemousse reached for the wine list and under the pretence of studying it unfolded the paper. The note was short and to the point. It said, quite simply, in large anonymous letters: MUST SEE YOU. CAN'T WAIT. SUGGEST RENDEZ-VOUS.'

He thought for a moment and then, entering into the spirit of the game, took out his pen and added a suitable reply in like hand. The only rendez-vous he could think of without going into great complications was his own room later that night.

He signalled to Felix. 'Tell the sommelier I will have a bottle of the Cornas,' he said in a loud voice.

'See that the note is returned,' he added quietly. 'It is inside the wine list; near the front—in the champagne section.'

'A wise choice, Monsieur, if I may say so. It will go well with your meal.' Felix gave his approval with scarcely a change of expression as he took the wine list. 'I will leave it for him in reception.'

Shortly afterwards he disappeared out of the dining room. He wasn't a moment too soon, for no sooner had he returned than the couple rose from their seats.

As they passed by his table Giampiero's eyes flickered for a fraction of a second. Monsieur Pamplemousse gave an answering signal that all was well and then they were gone.

By leaning forward he was able to follow their progress. He breathed a sigh of relief as he watched Giampiero make his own way across the hall and take both a key and the note from a pigeon-hole to one side of the reception desk.

There was a moment's anxiety when the girl, showing signs of impatience, paused on the stairs and said something to him, but Giampiero had everything under control. One second the note was in his hand, the next it had gone. It was like a conjuring trick.

As they disappeared together up the main stairs Monsieur Pamplemousse turned his attention to a plate which had just arrived on his table. It bore a large slice of *Pâté de Canard*, made as only Auguste could make it, with white Bresse duck, white fillet of pork and foie gras.

The wine was all he'd been led to expect. It was dark. It must have been almost black when it was first made. It tasted of the hard work that had gone into it and it augured well for the *tian* to come. Monsieur Pamplemousse winced as he jotted down a few notes before his main course arrived. He wished he'd thought to apply a little padding beneath his freshly repaired trousers. The ladies in the *nettoyage* had been most intrigued and he'd had to concoct yet another story.

He gave the wine a gentle swirl in the glass to open it out a little more. It was good that Auguste had chosen a simple dish in response to his request for something out of the ordinary. It was a point in his favour. All too often restaurants with two Stock Pots were guilty of over-embellishment; of too great an addiction to the cream jug with their sauces. They had grown up in an age when rich sauces were part and parcel of *haute cuisine*, and in many cases they were so steeped in tradition they would probably never change their ways.

It was the younger generation of chefs who had tried to break away from tradition. More and more they were laying claim to a third Stock Pot—and deservedly so. Without succumbing to the worst excesses of *nouvelle cuisine*, where colour and presentation often took precedence over all else, many had returned to the recipes of their forefathers and a simplicity which was wholly admirable in a land which was rich in meat and fish and fresh vegetables. It was a move which won his wholehearted approval and the *tian* in front of him was a blissful example.

Monsieur Pamplemousse looked forward to observing Pommes Frites' views on the matter, although if the lip-smacking going on under the table was anything to go by, the result was a foregone conclusion.

Waving aside the offer of a second helping, he issued instructions for a portion to be kept warm until they retired; an unnecessary request since Pommes Frites' reactions were much sought after and appreciated everywhere they went. A clean plate and a satisfied licking of the whiskers were accolades in themselves.

His cheese over and done with, Monsieur Pamplemousse decided against a coffee and opted instead for a *tisane verveine* in his room. To be truthful he had eaten more than enough, and a couple of involuntary sneezes came as a warning sign that his liver needed something more than the Vichy water to keep it in good working order.

A turn round the square with Pommes Frites was indicated. Apart from anything else there was work to be done and he needed to marshal his thoughts. The attack earlier in the day had been worrying to say the least; the more so as he still wasn't sure who had been the prime target—himself or Giampiero. Although the latter had brushed it aside at the time, there was something in his manner which didn't ring quite true. It crossed his mind that Giampiero might even have wanted to be followed that morning.

As they left the hotel he took a look around. It was already dark. A few people were taking their coffee on the hotel terrace. On the other side of the square the sound of laughter came from the Café du Centre. Somewhere a radio blared forth and then just as quickly cut out again. It was replaced by a rasping sound. Metal against metal. That, too, stopped again as suddenly as it had begun. Monsieur Pamplemousse was too old a hand to feel nervous, but there was a noticeable quickening of his step as he set off, carefully avoiding the shadowy areas of the little streets leading from either side of the Hôtel de Ville.

His feelings were obviously shared by Pommes Frites. After his nasty experience with the bush he directed his activities very pointedly at man-made objects, such as the fountain in the middle of the square. Pommes Frites was definitely off nature for the time being. After his nasty experience that morning even the plane trees surrounding the *boules* area were objects of suspicion. You knew where you were with stone. Stone stayed where it had been put.

His inspection and the call of nature complete, Pommes Frites took a last sniff and then led the way very firmly round the back of the hotel towards the kitchens. He felt hungry and supper was long overdue. Unlike some people, he only had two meals a day—give or take a snack or two in between.

Monsieur Pamplemousse undid the boot of his 2CV, removed a small canvas bag and metal cylinder, and connected the two together with a length of flexible tubing. He turned a knob on the cylinder, there was a hiss of escaping air, and seconds later a miniature house began to take shape, emerging from its container like a butterfly shedding its cocoon.

A deft tug at a zip fastener holding the front door in place, the spreading of a blanket on the floor, and the kennel was complete and ready for occupation.

As if on cue, a waiter emerged from the back of the hotel carrying a bowl containing the remains of the *tian* and another full of water. Soon Pommes Frites was busy with his supper.

Monsieur Pamplemousse knew better than to interrupt. From the expression on his face it was clear that Auguste's choice met with Pommes Frites' approval, and after a brief good-night pat on the head, he left him to it and turned back inside.

Pommes Frites' kennel was a great boon. The invention of a rubber specialist in Paris, who normally devoted his talents to more esoteric items, it made travelling around France much less of a problem than it might have been. Not all hotels welcomed dogs, and some charged accordingly. It also saved the embarrassment of having Pommes Frites suffer the indignity of being 'relegated' to the back of the car, as had sometimes happened in the early days. There were some things in life that were hard to explain to a dog. There was also the fact that after a heavy meal Pommes Frites was apt to snore rather loudly and, much as he loved him, sharing a room was not always the happiest of arrangements.

Closing the door behind him, Monsieur Pamplemousse made his way to the reception desk in order to collect his room key and to see if there was any mail.

Drawing a blank as far as mail was concerned, he picked up his key from the receptionist, confirmed his order for the *tisane* and turned to go upstairs, treading warily round some buckets and other paraphernalia left by the builders who were doing things to the downstairs facilities.

As he did so he became aware of some sort of activity going on in the little room which served as an office for Madame Sophie Douard.

Under the pretence of getting himself entangled with the handle of a bucket, Monsieur Pamplemousse gazed at Madame Douard in astonishment. Hidden from the watchful eye of the receptionist, she was standing just inside the doorway to her room and behaving in the most extraordinary manner. Both hands behind her neck, rather as if she was searching for something she had dropped down the back of her dress, she was rolling her eyes and running her tongue round her lips as if in the throes of some kind of a fit. For a moment he was irresistibly reminded of the seduction scene from a very bad film, then just as quickly he dismissed the thought. It was unthinkable.

He had never given the slightest cause for such behaviour.

Madame Sophie was probably having trouble with her zip fastener—either that or she'd had a bad attack of hiccups and had been trying to cure it by means of a cold key down her back. He was about to offer to go to her assistance when there was the sound of voices heading their way. Almost immediately Madame Douard sprang into action. Removing her hands from behind her neck, she straightened her dress and pushed the door shut with one swift movement.

By that time Monsieur Pamplemousse's problems with the bucket had become very real. All the same, in the brief moment between first hearing the voices and the slamming of the door, he could have sworn she'd winked at him. Moreover, it had been no ordinary wink, confined merely to the closing of one eye. It had been a full-blooded, no-holds-barred, voluptuous, uninhibited wink of a kind he'd only previously encountered during his days on the beat in some of the seamier areas of the Paris underworld, when invitations to stray from the straight and narrow had been many and varied.

And yet, even that was not a true analogy, for there had also been a certain childlike innocence about the whole thing which had totally removed all trace of lewdness.

'Are you all right, Monsieur?' He suddenly realised the waiter with the *tisane* was standing behind him.

Reflecting that there was nothing in the world so strange as people, Monsieur Pamplemousse led the way upstairs. His note-book was waiting for him. Before dinner he had begun the painstaking task of carrying out some running repairs and he was anxious to complete them before the night was out.

Thanking the waiter, he lifted the tiny pot from

its charcoal burner and poured himself a cup, savouring the sweet smell as he did so.

The more he examined his note-book the more he realised how lucky he was to have escaped so lightly. The pages looked as if they had been ravaged by some wood-boring beetle. He shuddered to think of the agony he would have had to endure had those same holes been in his leg. The few pieces of shot that had by-passed the leather cover of the book had only been peripheral, but had he caught the full blast . . . it didn't bear thinking about.

He became so absorbed in his task he soon forgot not only Madame Douard's strange antics but his appointment with Giampiero.

It wasn't until a sharp, metallic knock on the door brought him down to earth that he remembered it.

'One moment.' He hastily hid the pages under the bedcover. It wouldn't do for them to be seen.

But he needn't have worried. Giampiero hardly glanced at the bed as he entered the room. After a brief exchange of greetings he crossed to the balcony and looked outside for a moment. The moon was already high and as he stood silhouetted against the sky Monsieur Pamplemousse suddenly realised where he'd seen his face before. Or rather, to be more exact, where he'd seen a reasonable facsimile. It had been on his plate the previous evening. There was the same curly hair, the same Italian features.

As if reading his thoughts, Giampiero turned back into the room.

'You realise, of course, that it is me they are after, not you?'

'They?'

Giampiero gave a gesture of impatience. 'They . . . him . . . it . . . what does it matter? Had Eva and I been sitting where you sat last night you would have been spared the experience. I've been thinking about it all day. That man in the bushes this morning. Had it not been for your dog, who knows where the blast would have landed?' He glanced down at Monsieur Pamplemousse's legs. 'You are all right?'

'A mere flesh wound. It is nothing.'

'More like a bark wound, I should have thought.' Giampiero laughed. It struck Monsieur Pamplemousse that he sounded slightly drunk. Either that or he was nervous about something. He chose to ignore the remark, which he thought was slightly lacking in taste anyway.

'But why should they . . . he . . . it . . . be after you?'

Giampiero shrugged. 'The money, I suppose.'

'Money?'

'The only good thing about my accident . . . the insurance . . . a record sum. It took a long time, mind. At first there was a great deal of discussion. It was bad enough after the first accident, but later, when I had the second, there were all kinds of legal arguments. They even tried to say I only did it for the sake of the insurance.' He gave a shrill laugh. 'They should try putting themselves in my place. Fortunately I had a sympathetic judge. Now I am waiting for the note.'

'The note?' Monsieur Pamplemousse began to feel the conversation was getting a little one-sided. 'What note?'

'Don't you see? These things that have happened. They are all warnings. I have thought about it. The plastic head last night . . . the shooting this morning. If they had really wanted to kill they would have used something more powerful than a shotgun.

'Next, there will be a note saying, "Pay up, or else . . ." If you want my advice you will leave as soon as possible.'

'I'm afraid that is not possible,' said Monsieur Pamplemousse firmly. 'Anyway, if it is you they are after I see no point.'

'All right, but don't say I didn't warn you.' Giampiero made as if to run a hand through his hair and then stopped just in time. 'I suppose I shall get used to it one day. I don't know what I would do without Eva. She has been marvellous. Despite everything, she married me. It is no life for a young girl.'

'You were engaged when it happened?'

'No . . . we didn't even know each other. We met by accident some while later.' Giampiero gave a wry smile. 'One of my better accidents as things turned out. But just lately . . . things have been different. We are always on the move. I can't seem to settle. I find myself skulking in corners . . . wanting to be alone. Sometimes I feel I would like to end it all . . .'

'You mustn't think such things.' Monsieur Pamplemousse broke in as he felt a wave of sympathy come over him. Really, it was almost like father and son. He wished he could reach out and embrace Giampiero. 'What has happened must make life very difficult, but not impossible. Think of Renoir . . . in his old age his hands were so gripped by rheumatics he had to have his brush tied to them in order to work . . . but such work. Take Van Gogh,' he continued, warming to his theme. 'He lost an ear, but he still carried on.'

Giampiero shot him a strange look. 'What difference did losing an ear make?'

'Well, it couldn't have been easy.' Monsieur Pamplemousse felt a trifle hurt.

'I know. You are right.' Giampiero went out on to the balcony again and gazed across the valley. 'We share the same view, you and I. Our room is a little further along. Eva noticed it last night. We saw you just before you went to bed. Every evening we stand on our own balcony and every evening I think, despite everything, it is good to be alive.' There was a metallic clunk as Giampiero suddenly leaned forward and gripped the railings. 'If I were to paint, that is . . .'

Monsieur Pamplemousse opened his mouth to interrupt. His mind was suddenly full of questions, but for the time being at least they were destined to remain unasked. Instead, he found himself staring at the spot where a moment before Giampiero had been standing.

He rushed to the balcony as the night air was rent by a loud howl; a howl which was a mixture of surprise, terror and almost total disbelief. Peering gingerly through the gap where a section of the rail had once been he saw Giampiero clambering unsteadily to his feet some ten or twelve feet below. He looked shaken but otherwise unharmed.

Beside him, Pommes Frites, obviously in a state of considerable shock, gazed unhappily at the remains of his kennel as, to the accompaniment of a long drawn-out sigh of escaping air, it sank slowly to the ground beneath the weight of the section of railing. From the look of things Pommes Frites had been even luckier to escape injury than Giampiero.

Monsieur Pamplemousse bent down and examined the balcony rail. Accident-prone though Giampiero undoubtedly was, and powerful though his mechanical hands must be, it was inconceivable that they could have cut through several centimetres of metal. A quick glance confirmed his suspicions. On either side of the gap, plainly visible in the light from his room, were two fresh saw-cuts, and on the stonework below there were traces of metal filings. As he stood up he felt rather than saw a movement from a balcony further along. But when he looked there was nothing to be seen. He looked over the edge of his own balcony again. The kitchens were in darkness, as was the rest of the hotel. Pommes Frites, having given voice to his feelings on the matter, was busy licking his wounds. Giampiero was looking up.

'Wait there,' he called, somewhat unnecessarily in the circumstances. Neither Pommes Frites nor Giampiero looked as if they had any immediate plans to go anywhere. 'I will be right down.'

As he made his way along the corridor leading to the back stairs Monsieur Pamplemousse noticed a chink of light coming from beneath a door at the far end where the Douards had their quarters. Otherwise there was no sign of life. No voices. No doors opening to see what had happened.

Incredibly, apart from the breaking of the metal and Pommes Frites' howl, the whole episode had taken place in almost complete silence. Miraculously, the kennel must have broken Giampiero's fall, otherwise it would undoubtedly have been far worse. Perhaps he had a lucky streak after all.

It was a shame about Pommes Frites' kennel. If the worst came to the worst he would have to come upstairs and spend the night under the bed. Not an ideal solution—especially after the *tian*. Auguste hadn't stinted himself with the beans.

As he turned to go down the stairs, Monsieur Pamplemousse glanced at the light again. He wondered if he should have knocked on the door in case he needed help, then decided against it. There would be tedious explanations.

It was a decision which, had he but known it, spared him yet another shock—at least for the time being. The light, as it happened, came from beneath the door to Madame Sophie's apartment, and despite the lateness of the hour, Madame Sophie was very definitely at home to callers. Not to put too fine a point on it, had Monsieur Pamplemousse entered her room at that moment the chances of him making the ground floor before daybreak would have been very remote indeed. As it was he went on his way, blissfully unaware of his narrow escape.

Freshly bathed and powdered, Madame Sophie stood in the centre of her boudoir, contemplating her reflection in a massive carved giltwood framed mirror with an air of satisfaction.

True, there were a few odd wrinkles here and there, a line or two etched in beneath her chin, but on the whole nature and the passing of the years had been more than kind to her.

In the warm glow from the pink-shaded lamps which dotted the room, with its thick carpeting, its Louis Quatorze furnishings, its chintz curtainings, its silk hangings, and its massive four-poster bed, Madame Sophie bore a striking resemblance to her distant relative in the square outside. But there the likeness ended, for Hortense was made of stone; cold, hard and unyielding stone, and there was nothing cold, hard or unyielding about Madame Sophie at that particular moment.

As she reached forward to open a drawer in her tulipwood *table de toilette*, her flesh vibrated like a pink blancmange. Allowing a moment or two for it to settle down again, she removed the golden head of Queen Alexandra from one of a pair of Stanley Hall of London silver perfume jars—a present from a past admirer, an English visitor whose stay at La Langoustine had been enriched by an unexpected bonus over and above those already mentioned in his travel brochure, one for which even Monsieur Michelin would have been hard put to find a suitable symbol. Adding a touch of scent here, another two or three there, Madame Sophie began putting the finishing touches to her toilette in places which might have made the figure depicted on the other half of the set raise one if not both of his royal eyebrows.

Her fumigations complete, she addressed herself to an array of undergarments laid out on her bed, chose a black, silk *porte-jarretelles* and then, with a total disregard for the film of powder which every movement of her ample buttocks distributed around her, seated herself on a Falconnet giltwood canapé and proceeded to draw on a pair of black silk stockings with an air of loving care given only to those for whom work is also a pleasure and a joy.

For a moment or two she considered the possibility of donning a matching pair of hand-embroidered knickers, then tossed them to one side as being an unnecessary gilding of the lily. If all went well she would only have to take them off again and she would need all her energy.

Crossing to her dressing table, Madame Sophie pulled open another drawer and took out a small package purchased that very evening from the local *bricolage*. After first making sure it was folded inside out, she slipped it beneath the top of the *jarretelles* and stood for a moment running her hand sensuously up and down the polished surface of a carved mahogany standard lamp, savouring its every curve. A deep sigh escaped her lips. Already she could feel the blood coursing through her veins; blood that had been still for far too long, several weeks in fact.

For what seemed like the hundredth time that evening, she picked up the note she had found lying on the floor outside her office where it had fallen and ran her eyes over the words—even though she knew them off by heart. 'MUST SEE YOU. CAN'T WAIT. SUGGEST RENDEZ-VOUS. MY ROOM WHEN COAST CLEAR. P.'

The writer had obviously been hard put to contain his excitement as he penned the billet doux, for towards the end the writing began to change. Letters that had started off firm and bold became almost spidery as the hand trembled.

There was only one 'P' staying at the hotel. The 'P' who, on retiring to bed that evening had ordered a *tisane verveine*, which, as everyone knew, was noted for its aphrodisiacal effects. Who would have thought it? Still waters ran deep. All the times he had stayed at the hotel and never a word; hardly a glance even. That same 'P' who had become so over-excited earlier that evening he'd stepped in a bucket of whitewash.

Ignoring the incongruity of white upon black, Madame Sophie slipped into an embroidered silk nightdress, ran her tongue over lips already moist with anticipation and headed for the door.

If Mohammed was too shy to come to the mountain, the mountain certainly had no inhibitions whatsoever about visiting Mohammed. She had never been to bed with a wooden-legs before. It was an opportunity too good to be missed.

A moment later, like a galleon in full sail, she set off down the corridor carrying all before her with an air of regal splendour which would not have disgraced Madame de Pompadour herself.

4

TUESDAY NIGHT

POMMES FRITES STIRRED UNEASILY IN HIS sleep as a creaking in the corridor outside Monsieur Pamplemousse's room entered his subconscious and nudged him into wakefulness.

One way and another he hadn't been enjoying a very good night. When the bombshell in the shape of Giampiero landed on top of him he'd been in the middle of a particularly good dream—all about an inexhaustible supply of bones he'd discovered in a cave in the Dordogne. To have it broken into before he'd had a chance to take so much as one bite let alone hide any away for future use was bad enough, but then to see his kennel, his pride and joy, collapse before his very eyes—that was the end.

He'd tried giving the nozzle at the back a few hopeful chews, as he'd seen his master do on the odd occasion when the supply of compressed air had given out, but blowing into it was quite beyond his powers and in the end he'd given it up as a bad job, resigning himself to having to spend the rest of the night indoors.

Pommes Frites wasn't too keen on sleeping indoors during the summer months. The winter was a different matter entirely. During the winter it was nice being able to snuggle up in a warm bedroom close to the radiator. But there was nothing to equal waking early on a summer's morning and enjoying the freedom of a pre-breakfast stroll before anyone else was around. He would also miss the little titbits Monsieur Douard invariably brought him before he left for the market. The morsel of *Boeuf en Croûte* that morning had been especially nice; he almost preferred it cold. It had been one of the few good things about a day that had got steadily worse as it progressed.

Apart from that, rooms were inclined to be stuffy; you couldn't go to sleep with your head sticking out of the door as you could in a kennel. They were even more stuffy when you were expected to sleep under the bed; especially, it had to be said, when the bed belonged to someone like his master. Monsieur Pamplemousse didn't let little things like other people falling from balconies disturb his routine and he'd fallen asleep almost as soon as his head had touched the pillow. And once asleep, Monsieur Pamplemousse was inclined to snore. Tonight was no exception.

Then there was the question of the pain across his middle. Pommes Frites wasn't sure whether it had to do with Giampiero landing on top of his kennel, or whether it was something he'd eaten. It might have been the *tian*. There had been rather a lot of that. Or it could have been the soufflé dish he'd been given to lick clean. Whoever ordered the soufflé obviously had eyes that were bigger than their stomach. There had been a lot left over. It was unlikely to have been the pâté—rich though that had been. Nor the *Carré d'Agneau* he'd had for lunch—he could have eaten two lots of that and then come back for more if his master hadn't got there first. As for breakfast—that was much too long ago, and anyway breakfast didn't really count as a meal.

That was another thing about being outside. When you were outside and not feeling very well there were usually blades of grass to eat. Pommes Frites was a great believer in blades of grass as an antidote to all ills. Not that there was much in the way of green grass in St. Castille at that time of the year, but it was better than nothing.

He pricked up his ears again. He could definitely hear creaks in the corridor; creaks and heavy breathing. They seemed to be coming from right outside the door. By now he was thoroughly awake.

Normally Pommes Frites would have been on his feet and investigating the matter in a brace of shakes, but he suddenly realised that he was quite literally pinned to the floor. The pain in his stomach came not from its having been landed on earlier in the night, nor from an over-indulgence of the good things in life during the day. It came about because there was a large bulge in the mattress above him; a bulge in the shape of his master.

Wriggling was possible, if slightly painful; bounds were definitely out of the question.

Pommes Frites closed his eyes again and hoped that the noises, whatever they were, would go away. But he was doomed to disappointment.

A faint click from the direction of the door heralded a welcome draught of fresh air. It was followed almost immediately by another click and as the door closed there came a strong smell of talcum powder and he heard the sound of breathing again, closer this time and much heavier, then a soft rustle of silk as something white and filmy landed on the floor beside him.

Pommes Frites blinked at the object in astonishment, but before he had time to work out what was going on let alone do anything about it, the breath was suddenly knocked clean out of him for the second time that night as a heavy weight landed on top of the bed.

But if Pommes Frites was taken by surprise, Monsieur Pamplemousse was positively devastated. Unlike Pommes Frites, he was unable to claim that he'd been in the middle of a particularly pleasant dream; rather the reverse. He'd fallen asleep with a confusion of thoughts in his mind; thoughts which eventually began to form themselves into a small cloud on the horizon. A cloud which then turned and began to head in his direction, growing inexorably larger and all-enveloping with every passing second. Seconds, which at the time seemed like hours, but which he realised afterwards were all contained within the brief period between sleep and waking.

All he was aware of was a dreadful feeling of trying desperately to raise his leaden arms to ward off the cloud and being unable to move them. As he forced open his eyes, heavy with sleep, he realised to his horror that somewhere along the line the dream had turned into reality and that the amorphous mass on top of him had taken on human shape. A shape which was at once warm, voluptuous and all-embracing. A shape whose lips were showering him with endearments as they sought his own. Moist, sensuous, urgent lips, belonging to a body which seemed to possess more than its fair share of hands; hands which caressed and searched and stroked and squeezed.

Taking advantage of a momentary lull in the proceedings as his assailant raised herself and drew breath for an instant, Monsieur Pamplemousse managed to free one arm. Reaching out in desperation to the table beside his bed, he grasped the first thing that came to hand—a heavy, carved wooden candlestick.

No one would be able to say he'd gone down without a struggle.

But the moment of respite was short-lived. Before he had time to transfer his grip from the base to the top in order to make better use of it as a weapon, he felt himself being embraced yet again. Limbs stretched out, pinning both his arm and the candlestick between them.

Monsieur Pamplemousse steeled himself for a second assault, racking his brains as he did so for an explanation as to who his assailant might be and what possible circumstances could have triggered off such a bizarre event.

But the assault never came. True, the moans and groans and the intermittent cries of ecstasy continued unabated, but they had taken on a more regular pattern. He realised with a start that the pleasure being enjoyed by his intruder was not of his making, nor indeed was it of a kind that in his wildest and most boastful dreams could he possibly have emulated. Lying there, gathering his senses, Monsieur Pamplemousse had to admit to a faint feeling of regret that he was unable to share in the obviously all-pervading delight being enjoyed by his companion. For one wild moment he contemplated a little sleight of hand; a substitution of instruments. Then he dismissed the idea. In his present state of shock he would never get away with it. Far better to lie back and let matters take their course.

At last the movement ceased and with a long drawn-out gasp his visitor collapsed panting by his side.

'*Chéri.*' The whispering voice on the pillow beside him brought him to his senses with a bump. He suddenly realised where he'd heard it before.

'Never . . . never, never, never have I experienced such a moment. Such . . . love . . . such . . . manhood. I didn't realise it could be possible. If only I had known before. When I got your note . . .'

Monsieur Pamplemousse's mind raced ahead of the words. Note? What note? He had sent no note.

As the arms entwining him relaxed he took advantage of the moment and shifted his position.

Madame Douard appeared to be searching for something. Whatever it was she seemed to have found it, for she relaxed again. 'My little wooden legs . . .' her voice took on a girlish note as she turned to him again. 'Let me caress them in my own special way . . .'

Any doubts Monsieur Pamplemousse might have had as to what was going to happen next were resolved as a searing pain suddenly shot up his leg.

Merde upon *merde*! It could not be true. It was

not possible. The pain hit him again. This time a little higher up. It *was* true! Madame Douard was sandpapering his right leg! By the feel of it the paper was *très gros* quality at the very least.

Summoning all his strength, he gave a tremendous heave and leapt out of the bed, crossing to the door in a single bound, determined at any costs to escape the clutches of this daughter of the Borgias.

Once outside he hurried down the corridor as fast as his legs would carry him. Mindful of the fact that Madame Douard's knowledge of the hotel was infinitely greater than his, he took the stairs leading down into the hall two at a time and headed towards the toilets. Surely, inflamed with passion though she was, Madame Douard couldn't possibly follow him into the *Hommes*.

Rounding a corner, he narrowly missed the pile of builders' material and paused in order to peer up at the doors, trying to decipher in the dim glow of the emergency night lighting which was which. It was a long time since he'd used them.

As part of its modernisation, La Langoustine's public toilets were undergoing extensive changes. A feature which obviously gave Monsieur Douard particular pride when he'd been describing it over breakfast was the installation of a system of automatic flushing in the *Hommes*, operated by means of an electric beam. All very well, but in the circumstances he wished they'd devoted a little more of the money to buying some proper symbols for the doors. In the half-light it was hard to tell whether he was looking at a man wearing an extra long jacket or a girl in a very short dress.

He was about to give up and take a chance

when he noticed a relic of earlier times which had yet to be removed; some carved wooden letters high up on the door which spelled out the word 'ADA'. By process of elimination, the second door along had to be the one he wanted. A moment later he was safely inside.

As the door closed behind him he looked around and saw facing him a long shelf, surmounted by a mirror, running the length of one wall, and below it a row of hand-basins and stools.

Gazing at his reflection in the mirror, Monsieur Pamplemousse realised several things in quick succession. First of all, in his haste he had come away without his pyjamas. Not that there would have been either the time or the opportunity for such niceties. The weather was warm and they were still in his suitcase. Second, also reflected in the mirror, was a long line of cubicles, but nowhere was there any sign of the urinals Auguste had described so graphically that morning.

His heart sank. He was in the *Dames* after all. *Merde!*

The appositeness of the expression suddenly struck him. At any other time it might have brought a smile to his lips, but he froze as he heard the sound of footsteps approaching. High heels on stone flooring. On the principle of any port in a storm he made a dive for the nearest cubicle. Pushing the door shut behind him he collapsed on to the seat and held his breath. He wondered whether or not to risk drawing the bolt and then decided to play it by ear and await developments.

The outside door opened and swung gently to again. He caught a faint whiff of perfume. The smell was expensive, discreet, subtle. Whoever it belonged to it certainly wasn't Madame Sophie; he would remember hers for a long time to come. The wearer was obviously looking for something. He heard a murmur of impatience as a cupboard door was opened and then closed again. He felt his heart miss a beat as the footsteps came in his direction and paused, then he relaxed again as they entered the next cubicle along.

He waited gloomily for further developments. It was the Follies all over again. No one would believe him a second time if he said he'd gone through the wrong door by mistake. He would be branded as a Peeping Tom for ever. He could almost see the headlines. NUDE INTRUDER STRIKES AGAIN!

He pricked up his ears. Whatever else was happening in the next cubicle he was sufficiently a man of the world to realise that it didn't point to the occupant having been taken short.

There was a heavy clunk which sounded like someone removing the top from the cistern. A moment later there was a splash followed by an even heavier clunk as the top was replaced. After a moment's pause there came the sound of rushing water as the toilet was flushed.

After what seemed like an interminable wait while the cistern refilled the cubicle door opened again. There was a rustle from the paper-towel dispenser, the sound of a wastebin lid being lifted, a faint squeak from the outer door, then the clip clop of feet as whoever it was disappeared again as swiftly as she had come.

Monsieur Pamplemousse waited for a moment or two, counting his lucky stars that he had remained undiscovered, then gingerly pushed open his cubicle door. Something very odd was going on and he was determined to get to the bottom of it.

Mindful of his narrow escape, he decided to make sure the coast was clear before going any further. It wouldn't do for whoever had been in there to return and catch him red-handed.

Opening the door to the corridor he stuck his head through the gap and peered out. All was quiet.

He was about to withdraw inside again when he felt rather than saw a pair of eyes boring into him. Focusing his gaze on the far side of the entrance hall he became aware of a faint glow from a lighted cigarette, and below it, merging into the darkness of a deep armchair, a figure in uniform.

'*Bonne nuit!*' Much to his annoyance, Monsieur Pamplemousse realised his voice was a shade higher than he'd intended. He cleared his throat and pointed up to the sign. 'I seem to have made a mistake. It is not easy in the dark.'

The figure in the armchair didn't move. There was a sucking noise, almost like a sigh, and the cigarette momentarily glowed brighter. From its light Monsieur Pamplemousse made out the by now familiar figure of the gendarme. He stifled his annoyance. He'd totally forgotten about the gendarme.

Summoning all his dignity, he emerged from the toilet and headed back towards the stairs, conscious as he did so of a pair of eyes watching his every movement.

As he reached the first floor landing he quickened his pace. The possibility of meeting anyone else at that time of night was slight, all the same . . . he paused outside his door and listened. Suppose Madame Sophie was still there, awaiting him with open arms? *Mon Dieu!* What a night!

Bending down, he applied his eye to the keyhole and then realised that it was a waste of time. The light was still off. As he stood up he caught a glimpse of a uniformed figure at the top of the stairs. It ducked out of sight, leaving behind a trail of cigarette smoke.

Taking the bull by the horns, he flung open the door and marched deliberately into his room, reaching for the light switch at the same time. As the room flooded with light a form on the bed lifted its head and stared at him reproachfully through eyes red from lack of sleep.

'Pardon!' Monsieur Pamplemousse flicked the switch which operated the lights over the dressing table and then turned off the overhead ones. In all the excitement he'd forgotten about Pommes Frites. But from the look on his face it was clear that Pommes Frites had not forgotten his master.

The whole disastrous evening was imprinted for ever more, not only on Pommes Frites' mind, but on most of his body as well. One way and another it had taken quite a battering that night. Having his kennel collapse on top of him had been bad enough, but that had all been over in a matter of seconds. Being incarcerated under the bed had been much, much worse—never-endingly worse. The combined weight of his master and Madame Sophie had strained the springs to their utmost and when the activity was at its height it had felt for all the world as if he'd been trapped beneath a giant pile driver.

Pommes Frites had no wish to pass judgment on

the morals of others, least of all his master, but he wished they'd carried out their frolickings elsewhere.

Battered and bruised, when the coast was clear and he was at last able to crawl out from his hiding place, Pommes Frites sought refuge on top of the bed. There he intended to stay until he was removed by force. Not that he felt totally safe even then. He wouldn't have been at all surprised if the ceiling suddenly fell in. Nothing would have surprised him any more.

At least . . . he fixed his master with a stare. He had been expecting some kind of an apology, a word of cheer or a friendly pat, but Monsieur Pamplemousse obviously had his mind set on other things. During the course of their life together he, Pommes Frites, had been witness to many strange goings on. Had he been equipped for the task he could have written a book about them. A book which might well have reached the best sellers list in *Animal Ways*, but . . . he blinked in order to make sure he was seeing aright—never before had he seen his master acting quite so strangely.

Suddenly aware of Pommes Frites' unwinking gaze, Monsieur Pamplemousse turned his back on him. Pommes Frites had a very disconcerting gaze when he chose and he wasn't in the mood for explanations; he had enough problems as it was.

Madame Douard's shapely form, fashioned by nature in one of her more generous moods, had been made even more luxurious over the years by its owner's pursuit of good food. The two combined meant that the nightdress she had left behind fitted him like a glove. And like a glove, putting it on was not as easy as it looked—especially as he didn't want to run the risk of damaging it irreparably in the process. Bending over would be hazardous in the extreme.

However, something untoward had taken place in the *Dames* and he was determined to get to the bottom of it before the night was very much older.

Taking a large, white handkerchief out of a drawer, he tied a knot in each corner and then slipped it over his head like a makeshift bonnet.

'Good boy!' With a reassuring wave to Pommes Frites he made for the door and hurriedly shut it behind him.

'*Good boy!*' Pommes Frites stared suspiciously at the closed door for quite a long while. He was used to the various nuances in his master's voice, and the guilt-ridden tones of the last remark had not escaped him. It was the kind of voice Monsieur Pamplemousse usually reserved for Madame Pamplemousse on those occasions when he arrived home late without a reasonable excuse, reasonable in Madame Pamplemousse's eyes, that is ... Part apologetic, part defiant, with a dash of apprehension mixed in for good measure.

Pommes Frites heaved a deep sigh. In his haste his master hadn't even bothered to turn out the light.

He was about to try and resume his slumbers when something else happened to delay matters. A piece of blue paper came sliding underneath the door. A piece of blue paper, moreover, which had a border of flowers round it. Even without moving Pommes Frites could see them: large brightly coloured flowers. Also without moving he could smell a scent; a scent which he recognised at once. It belonged to the other half of the two people most responsible for his present aches and pains.

Pommes Frites tensed himself lest the paper should be a prelude to yet another attack, perhaps this time on his own person. Then he relaxed again as he caught the sound of retreating footsteps going back down the corridor.

Unaware of the happenings on the floor above, Monsieur Pamplemousse made his way towards the toilets in a curious crablike shuffle. Negotiating the stairs had taken rather longer than he'd bargained for, partly on account of his having to take them very carefully one at a time lest he burst the seams of Madame Sophie's nightdress, but also—although he wouldn't have admitted it to anyone—wearing it was having a delayed but pronounced effect on his ardour.

He toyed with the idea of assuming a disguised voice and saying good night to the gendarme, then he rejected it. That might be pushing things a little too far. In any case the man seemed to have disappeared for the time being.

Breathing a sigh of relief, he pushed open the door to the *Dames*, noting as he did so the outline symbol on the door and above that the original sign 'EVE'. It wouldn't do to make a second mistake and compound the felony by getting himself trapped in the *Hommes* dressed in his present garb.

Once inside he lost no time. Making straight for the cubicle where all the activity had taken place, he lifted the top from the cistern and peered inside.

A look of satisfaction came over his face. Clearly visible at the bottom was a long piece of metal with a polished wooden handle. Pulling up a sleeve of the nightdress, he reached down into the water. It was as he'd suspected; a small, single-ended saw, equipped with a fine-toothed blade of the type used for cutting metal. The blade, which was new, bore signs of having recently been used. Its blueness had been worn away and fragments of metal clogged the middle section of teeth.

Wrapping the handle in a piece of toilet paper, he laid it carefully on the floor while he replaced the cistern top. Then he picked it up again, unbolted the cubicle door and made for the exit. Altogether, he could hardly have been in there for more than a minute or two.

'*Bonsoir*, Pamplemousse.' He jumped as a familiar figure detached itself from a pillar in the hall and came towards him.

'Or should I say, *bonjour*?' Inspector Banyuls gazed at him coldly. Making no attempt to hide the contempt in his voice, he looked Monsieur Pamplemousse slowly up and down, taking in the saw as he did so. The construction he placed on the meeting was obvious. A saw was for cutting wood. Holes cut in wood were for looking through.

He turned to the gendarme. 'You did well to call me, Lesparre. But as it is late I suggest we leave further enquiries until morning. As for you . . .' He turned back to Monsieur Pamplemousse and held out his hand. 'I will relieve you of that, if I may.'

'Now, look here.' Monsieur Pamplemousse made a half-hearted attempt at bluster. 'Before we go any further I suggest you question your subordinate on who else has used the toilet within the last half-hour. I am not the only one.'

'Is this true?'

The gendarme gave an indifferent shrug. 'How should I know? I have my rounds to do. I have seen this man twice. Once as naked as the day he was born, and now . . .' He left the sentence unfinished, but his opinion on the whole sordid matter was all too obvious.

Monsieur Pamplemousse knew better than to argue. He had met the type many times before in his career. Fine if they were on your side, but there was no getting through if they weren't.

'All right.' He handed the saw to Inspector Banyuls, who tucked it inside his jacket with an air of satisfaction. 'But it could be to your advantage to have it checked for finger-prints as soon as possible. With luck the water may not have destroyed them, in which case you will find other ones than mine on the handle.

'As for my being here in the first place, you will no doubt be aware of the fact that certain alterations are taking place. Obviously the toilet facilities for the *Dames* are being enlarged. That is why they now have two rooms. One,' he pointed to the sign on the door he'd just come out of, 'one is marked "EVE" and the other "ADA". Naturally, when I first saw the one marked "ADA" I assumed this one was for the men. It is a mistake anyone might make.'

He was pleased he had treated the matter in a dignified way. Others might have tried to think up a cock-and-bull story. It paid to tell the truth in the end.

Inspector Banyuls was looking at something on the floor. He followed the direction of his gaze and dimly made out a small piece of carved wood.

'I'm sorry. I don't have my glasses and unfortunately I am unable to bend down at the moment.'

'Boasting again, Pamplemousse!' The inspector

bent down, picked up the object and held it in the air between thumb and forefinger.

It was obvious what it was, but clearly he was determined to get his pound of flesh.

'I am surprised that an ex-member of the Sûreté should be so easily taken in,' he said. 'I think you will find, although I am sure you already know, that the toilets are as they have always been . . . "ADAM" and "EVE". It is simply that the letter "M" has fallen off the end of the "ADAM".

'Also,' he added, pressing home his point remorselessly, 'next time you feel an overwhelming desire to dress up as a woman, I suggest you either confine your activities to your own room or you first shave off your moustache. It does not go well with your costume.'

Monsieur Pamplemousse reached instinctively to his face and then, conscious of a barely suppressed snigger from the gendarme, turned on his heels. He knew when he was beaten.

Aware this time of not one, but two pairs of eyes boring into him, he made his way slowly back up the stairs. Halfway up the worst happened. Over-reaching his step, he felt the material start to give. The sound of tearing silk echoed round the hall, but he was determined not to give the others the satisfaction of seeing him hurry. Never had a flight of stairs seemed so long.

As he let himself wearily into his room he caught sight of the note on the floor and, regardless of the harm he was doing to the rest of the nightdress, bent down to pick it up.

'My shy one of the darkness,' he read. 'You have no need to run away as you did tonight. You have made me the happiest woman in the whole world. Sleep well, and gather your strength for the morrow. I will make sure you have need of it. I shall be counting the seconds until we meet again. Your ever-loving, ever-wanting, ever-needing, ever-lusting . . . S.'

Too tired even to bother removing the nightdress, Monsieur Pamplemousse flopped down on the bed alongside Pommes Frites. Gazing up at the ceiling he offered up a silent prayer, thanking the good Lord that Sophie did not plan to return that night. At least it gave him some sort of respite. He glanced at the candlestick. Things were in a mess and no mistake. It would take some sorting out.

As he reached back over his head to turn out the light a warm tongue sought out his arm. He immediately felt better. There was something very reassuring about Pommes Frites' tongue in times of trouble.

In no time at all their snores mingled. Both were out for the count.

They were still in the same position when the chambermaid opened the door with her pass key next morning, illuminated by a shaft of sunlight sneaking in between a gap in the shutters.

Putting a hand to her mouth to stifle a scream, she stood in the doorway drinking in the scene. A dog—a large dog, and a man dressed in a woman's silk nightdress, ripped all the way down the back—and what was he clutching? A candlestick! *'Mon Dieu!'*

It was the kind of thing she had read about in *Dimanche-Soir,* but never in her wildest dreams had she expected to see such goings on at La Langoustine. In her time she'd come across many strange sights, but this one capped the lot. It had all the ingredients of a first-rate scandal. She would have something to tell the others when she got back home, my word she would!

Quietly, she closed the door behind her and turned the card on the handle to *occupé*.

5

WEDNESDAY MORNING

'*ATTENDEZ, S'IL VOUS PLAÎT.*' WITH THE BRIEF-
est of signals to Pommes Frites, Monsieur Pamplemousse entered the telephone booth outside the
Hôtel de Ville, placed a large pile of coins neatly on
one side of the shelf and a carefully folded copy of
Ici Paris on the other, then drew a deep breath as
he mentally prepared himself for the first of three
calls, all of which were, to a greater or lesser extent, of a confidential nature. The bedrooms of La
Langoustine were not yet equipped for direct dial-
ling and he had no wish to be listened-in to by the
girl in reception, still less Madame Douard if she
happened to be around.

The first of his calls was to his wife, Doucette.
He'd been having qualms of conscience about
Doucette. Doucette, who stayed at home looking
after the running of flat, doing the washing
and ironing, watering the plants, dusting, standing
in supermarket queues, while he, Pamplemousse,

was away on his travels—often for weeks or months at a time.

If only he could explain to her the loneliness of it all. The sheer boredom of having to eat meal after meal on behalf of *Le Guide* and its readers, some of whom probably couldn't tell a *Tivoli aux Fraises* from a *Bombe Surprise*. Awarding marks for a *sauce Béarnaise* one day, taking them away on the morrow for an overcooked *sauce Périgourdine*. Having to stuff himself with *Écrevisses à la Bordelaise* followed by *Pêches à l'Aurore*, when all he really craved for was a simple underdone steak and salad, with perhaps a *glace vanille* to round things off. She would never understand. The grass was always greener on the other side of the fence.

As the phone began to ring at the other end of the line he brushed a crumb from his coat sleeve and made a mental note to add croissants to the growing list of bonus points for the hotel.

Breakfast had been a little later than usual—mainly because in all the excitement he'd forgotten to leave his order card outside the bedroom door. But in the event it had been one of the most delicious croissants he'd eaten for a long time. Or, if he were to be absolutely honest, *three* of the most delicious croissants, for they had been very more-ish. Warm, buttery, with a satisfying lightness, they had positively melted in the mouth. A perfect accompaniment to the large glass of freshly squeezed orange juice and the slightly acrid but flavoursome coffee, not to mention the bowls of home-made *confiture*, the berries of which were as juicy and full of fruit as the day on which they had been picked; a miracle of preservation. Altogether a most rewarding start to the morning. The slice of lemon in Pommes Frites' water bowl had been a pleasant touch as well.

For a moment the memory of it all brought about another twinge of conscience and he toyed with the idea of asking his wife if she would care to join him for the rest of the stay. But only for a moment. A click as the receiver was lifted at the other end brought him sharply back to earth. In the circumstances such thoughts would never do. He had enough problems as it was. He must not weaken. He told himself Doucette would not enjoy the experience. Apart from all the undercurrents at work the rich food would play havoc with her diet.

'Couscous, is that you?' He put out a tentative endearment to test the water. '*Oui. Oui, oui, chérie,* it is I, Aristide . . . *Oui,* we are still in St. Castille . . . *Chérie,* how strange . . . I was only thinking to myself a moment ago how nice that would be, but unfortunately something important has come up . . . No, Doucette, I think it would be better if you didn't. Really, I do. I cannot explain for the moment, but I have to remain here a little longer, you understand? Besides, it is not like being on the coast and you know how much you dislike the cold. The mountain air . . .'

Holding the telephone receiver away from his ear, Monsieur Pamplemousse gazed at it distastefully. It was all too clear that Doucette didn't understand. He decided to play his trump card. The one that never failed.

'In that case, *chérie* . . . if you would *really* like to . . . I will make immediate arrangements. You can catch an afternoon train. I will arrange to have it met. You will be here by . . .'

The reaction was as he had predicted. How could

she possibly leave Paris when there was so much work to do? Who would take care of the flat? The *plombier* was arriving on Thursday to put a new washer on the kitchen tap—something he couldn't possibly do even if he was there to do it—which he wasn't. Besides, she was in the middle of making a new dress . . .

Monsieur Pamplemousse stifled his relief and allowed his attention to wander across the square. Even Pommes Frites seemed to have caught the general mood of the conversation, for he was standing bolt upright with his ears pricked and his legs wide apart as if ready for the off at a moment's notice.

'No, *chérie*, I do not know for how long. Perhaps it will be for one more day, perhaps two. Maybe a week.' He lowered his voice. 'It all depends.'

Almost immediately he regretted placing so much emphasis on the last phrase.

'No, no, no, Doucette, of *course* there is no other. I promise you on my honour, I have been faithful.'

Catching sight of a priest entering the church on the far side of the square, Monsieur Pamplemousse hastily crossed himself and turned back into the booth. Looked at in a certain light what he had just said was undoubtedly true. He, Pamplemousse, had been faithful. Faithfulness was largely a matter of intent. Was it his fault if others, less strong, had forced themselves on—or even *upon* him? Might it not be true to say that it was only consideration for others, a desire not to disturb them in their sleep by calling out, that had stifled his protests? The Americans, as ever, had a neat way of putting it. What was the expression they used? Brownie points. Did he not at the very least deserve a few Brownie points for his unselfishness?

'And how are the window boxes, Couscous?' he enquired. 'Have you given them plenty of water? You know how quickly they dry out in this hot weather . . . It is raining in Paris! how strange! Here the sun is shining. It is like . . .'

A loud click brought the conversation to an abrupt end—at least as far as Madame Pamplemousse was concerned.

Merde! Women! Monsieur Pamplemousse replaced the receiver with rather more force than he had intended and prepared himself for the second call of the morning.

It was brief and to the point.

'*Bonjour.* Pamplemousse here. May I have the office of Monsieur le Directeur, please?'

'Certainly, Monsieur Pamplemousse. At once, Monsieur Pamplemousse.'

'Chief, Pamplemousse here. I have a slight change of plans. It will necessitate a few more days in the area.

'Ah, you have already heard? A strange business. It was in the *Poularde de Bresse en Vessie.*

'Yes, chief. Thank you, chief.

'*Oui*, I will take care.'

'*Le Guide* needs you, Pamplemousse. You must be in Rouen by next Sunday at the latest. There is a deadline to meet. There have been bad reports of their *Mille-feuille de Saumon au Cerfeuil.* I would go myself but I cannot spare the time.' The directeur of *Le Guide* spoke in the clipped tones of a general preparing his troops for battle. Tones which, try as he might, Monsieur Pamplemousse always found hard not to imitate when they were holding a conversation.

Catching sight of an elderly woman peering at him through the glass he realised with a start that he had been standing rigidly to attention. Turning his back on her he tried to relax.

The truth of the matter was that the whole organisation of *Le Guide* was planned like a military operation. The walls of headquarters were covered in maps, each of which was festooned with flags. The operations room itself—the holy of holies, to which admittance was gained by green pass only—was staffed by uniformed girls who pushed little bronze figures around on giant tables with croupier-like efficiency. Monsieur Pamplemousse knew that provided he filled in the correct forms all would be well and his request granted, but woe betide him if his reports were late. It would mean some pretty heavy field-work in the weeks to come—possibly entailing two *dîners* a night. He blanched at the thought. Thank heaven for Pommes Frites.

'Hullo . . . Pamplemousse . . . are you there?'

'*Oui*, Monsieur le Directeur.' This would never do.

'My regards to Pommes Frites. Oh, and Pamplemousse . . . if you stay more than three days don't forget your P189.'

'*Oui*, Monsieur le Directeur. *Merci. Au revoir*, Monsieur le Directeur.'

Monsieur Pamplemousse replaced the receiver and mopped his brow. And now for the most delicate, and yet if he intended to stay another night in St. Castille, probably the most important call of the three. He took out his spectacles, wiped them clean, and checked a ringed number on page fifteen of *Ici Paris*—just to make doubly sure.

'*Poupées Fantastiques, à vôtre service.*' The voice at the other end sounded unctuous in the extreme; soft and oily, like an over-dressed aubergine. Monsieur Pamplemousse recognised it at once. It belonged to the proprietor, Oscar. Voice and owner matched perfectly. Nothing changed.

He cleared his throat. 'I wish to place an order,' he said briskly. 'I need it urgently so I am prepared to pay whatever is necessary.' That should do it.

'Certainly, Monsieur. One moment, Monsieur, while I find a pencil.'

Monsieur Pamplemousse began issuing his instructions. 'That is correct. The Mark IV. As advertised in *Ici Paris*. The de luxe model.'

'An excellent choice, Monsieur. I can assure you it is impossible to do better. Our customers are worldwide and we guarantee complete satisfaction. All our Mark IV models are individually tested before they leave our work rooms.'

Monsieur Pamplemousse suppressed a shudder. 'It is not for me . . .' he began.

He was interrupted by a fruity chuckle. 'That is what they all say, Monsieur. If I were to tell you the names of some of our clients . . . However, I can assure you of our complete discretion. All records of orders are in code and kept under lock and key.'

'I wish,' said Monsieur Pamplemousse, trying to sound as blasé as possible, 'for the male version. Battery driven, but with certain modifications.'

'Certain modifications?' Monsieur Pamplemousse almost felt the hand go over the mouthpiece at the other end. He took a deep breath.

'I would like it to have wooden legs.'

'*Wooden legs?*' The man seemed to take an unnecessary delight in repeating the words as slowly and loudly as possible. So much for the discretion of *Poupées Fantastiques*.

Monsieur Pamplemousse looked uneasily over his shoulder. The woman outside appeared to be doing something to her deaf aid. Probably turning up the volume.

'Is it or is it not possible?' he barked. The conversation had already gone on far too long for his liking.

'Monsieur, all things are possible. As you can see from our advertisement we cater for all tastes. Nothing is too bizarre or *exotique*. Although I have to admit . . . would this be for Madame?'

'No, it would not!' thundered Monsieur Pamplemousse. 'And another thing . . .'

'*Another?*' The man could hardly keep the excitement from his voice.

'I want delivery today.'

'Today? Monsieur is joking, of course.'

'Listen, you.' Monsieur Pamplemousse decided to play it rough. 'I said today and I mean today. I do not mean yesterday, nor do I mean tomorrow. There is a high-speed train leaving Paris at fourteen twenty-six hours. It should arrive in Orange at about eighteen hundred. I shall be there to meet it. If it is not on that train I shall take immediate steps to have your premises closed down and you with them. Now, do I make myself totally and absolutely clear or do I have to spell it out in words of one syllable?'

There was a long silence at the other end during which Monsieur Pamplemousse stole a quick glance at the outside world. The woman with the deaf aid was almost wetting herself with excitement. She had been joined by two others.

'What name shall I put on the parcel, Monsieur?'

'Pamplemousse.' He tried to speak as quietly as possible.

'Pamplemousse? Not *the* Monsieur Pamplemousse? Pamplemousse of the Sûreté?' A note of respect had entered the voice.

'*Late* of the Sûreté. An early retirement . . .' He wished now he had used a nom de guerre.

'Ah, yes . . .' A whistle came down the line. 'I remember now . . . there was all that trouble with the girls at the Follies. Thirty-three wasn't it?'

'Fifteen,' sighed Monsieur Pamplemousse.

'Tell me, Inspector.' Oscar began to regain some of his earlier confidence. 'What is she like? Do you have any photos? We pay good prices for the right kind of negatives.'

'The fourteen twenty-six TGV!' Monsieur Pamplemousse decided he had had enough. For the second time that morning he was about to slam the receiver down, then he had second thoughts.

'One more thing.'

'*Oui*, Inspector?'

'I would like a plastic inflatable dog kennel. King size.'

'A plastic inflatable *dog kennel . . . King size*? *Mon Dieu!*'

'If you consult your records you will find I purchased one some four years ago. I had it made specially.'

Monsieur Pamplemousse felt in a better mood as he left the telephone booth. His last request had clearly given him game, set and match.

'*Pardon,* Monsieur.' The woman with the deaf aid, her bloodless lips made ever thinner by being tightly compressed in disapproval, pushed past him and began ostentatiously cleaning the mouthpiece of the telephone with her handkerchief, much to the enjoyment of her friends.

Avoiding their gaze, Monsieur Pamplemousse looked around for Pommes Frites, but Pommes Frites was nowhere to be seen. That was all he needed. He could think of nothing he wanted to do less at that moment than hang about outside the telephone booth. Quite a small crowd had collected and they were eyeing him with a mixture of interest and downright disbelief.

Reaching into an inside pocket he withdrew a small whistle and blew into it hopefully several times.

His audience broke into a titter as they waited for the blast and none followed. Much to Monsieur Pamplemousse's embarrassment, Pommes Frites was clearly out of range. For a moment or two he toyed with the idea of trying to explain the basic principles of silent dog whistles to his audience, but then he thought better of it. They didn't look as if they would be terribly receptive. Instead, he pretended to study a poster in the window of the P.T.T. No doubt Pommes Frites would reappear in his own good time. He always did.

Unaware of his master's predicament, Pommes Frites made his way along the Grande Avenue Charles de Gaulle looking more than a little pleased with himself.

Not even one of his most ardent admirers—and he had a great many—would have credited him with an over-abundance of grey matter. Generosity, an unrivalled and highly developed sense of taste in matters culinary, a capacity for love and affection, steadfastness, tenacity; he had many things going for him. But when it came to such mundane matters as, for example, the putting of two and two together and making four, it took him a little while to get things sorted out in his mind. In short, equations were not one of his strong points. Simultaneous ones even less so.

On the other hand, by remaining blissfully unaware of his mathematical shortcomings he was able to sail through life without the additional worries such knowledge often brought to others.

Two and two could sometimes make five, at other times three; it depended entirely on circumstances. And in Pommes Frites' view it didn't really matter much anyway.

On this particular morning, however, there was a gleam in his eye and a resolute angle to his tail which showed beyond all shadow of doubt that he, Pommes Frites, had reached a decision. And once Pommes Frites reached a decision there was no diverting him. It was a decision, moreover, that had to do with the safety of his master. Than which, in his eyes, there could be no finer cause.

Nose to the ground, he ignored the rather tasty looking *tranche* of *Terrine de Sanglier* which Monsieur Hollard was placing in the *charcuterie* window to his right, turned a blind eye towards a ginger cat disappearing down an alleyway to his left, and closed his olfactory glands to the smell of freshly baked bread wafting down the street from Madame Charbonnier's *pâtisserie*.

Pausing only to leave his mark on a concrete

flower tub standing on a corner of the newly completed pedestrian precinct, he hurried on his way, following a trail which led him up some steps towards the Place Napoleon. There was a purposeful expression on his face; an expression which boded ill for anyone who attempted to get in his way without a very good reason.

It had taken Pommes Frites some little while to reach the conclusion that all was not well, and having reached that conclusion he was determined to do something about it.

The sound of Madame Pamplemousse's voice through the glass door of the telephone booth had set him worrying. There had been something in the tone of her voice, not to mention the way Monsieur Pamplemousse regarded the end of the telephone receiver as he held it out at arm's length, which pointed to the fact that 'something was up'. What happened shortly afterwards had clinched matters in his mind.

Pommes Frites knew several very good reasons why Monsieur Pamplemousse was reluctant to leave town; and one of those reasons, had his master but known, passed within two feet of him shortly after he entered the telephone booth.

The encounter had been a chance one, for the man in question reacted in a way which could only be described as furtive in the extreme. Pulling a black Homburg down over his forehead, he'd turned his back towards Monsieur Pamplemousse and crept past the telephone box until well clear, before disappearing up the Grande Avenue Charles de Gaulle as if his very life depended on it.

All of which, given the fact that it was a hot day and there were other equally interesting things happening in the square at the time, might not have occasioned anything more than a passing glance from Pommes Frites, had it not been for the smell; an unusually strong and clearly recognisable scent which set his nose twitching and made him jump to his feet with all his senses racing.

Not for nothing had Pommes Frites been born a bloodhound. Bloodhounds were good at smells and he'd met that same one before—to be precise, in, on and around the bush he'd encountered up the hill the previous morning, and it had remained firmly fixed in his memory ever since.

Apart from having a personal score to settle, he had a feeling he might be able to kill at least two birds with one bite—and he knew exactly where he intended placing it if he got half a chance. Hopefully, if all went well, he could also do something to put his master back in favour with Madame Pamplemousse. And with these thoughts uppermost in his mind, he set off in hot pursuit.

Not that Pommes Frites disliked Madame Pamplemousse. Her complaints regarding the amount of hairs he left behind when he rose from his afternoon nap had about as much effect on him as did water on a duck's back. Pommes Frites was not one to fly in the face of nature. There were things he could do something about and there were things he could do nothing about. Loose hairs happened to be something he could do nothing about. As for complaints about the state of his paws when he came indoors after a walk in the rain, people who worried about such trifles ought not to polish their floors. It was a matter of differing temperaments.

Monsieur Pamplemousse understood about such things. Monsieur Pamplemousse often came under fire himself for much the same reasons: crumpled cushions, stray hairs, muddied shoes. It was a case of like gravitating towards like and there was an understanding and a bond of affection between them that mere words could not describe.

Besides, Pommes Frites owed Monsieur Pamplemousse a great debt of gratitude.

It dated back to the occasion of Monsieur Pamplemousse's early retirement from the force.

It so happened that around the same time Pommes Frites, who'd been on attachment to the Eighteenth Arrondissement where Monsieur Pamplemousse lived, was made redundant following a government cut-back.

Although it was a simple matter of last in first out, it wasn't a nice thing to happen to a dog of Pommes Frites' sensibilities, especially so early on in his career. Trained to the peak of perfection, passing his course with flying colours, only to find himself discarded like an old slipper.

Word had reached Monsieur Pamplemousse, who'd rescued him in the nick of time from being sent to the local dogs' home; a journey from which there would probably have been no return.

A nicer retirement present Monsieur Pamplemousse couldn't have wished for, nor could Pommes Frites have dreamed of a happier turn of fate. It was the kind of thing a dog doesn't forget in a hurry.

All these and many other things might have entered Pommes Frites' mind that morning had he been given to deep and philosophical thoughts, and if he hadn't had his attention firmly fixed on more important things.

As it was he bounded up the remaining steps

leading to the Place Napoleon, ignored a sign which proclaimed that 'CHIENS' were 'INTERDITS', threaded his way in and out of the various stalls dotting the square, and hurried towards number 7-*bis* on the far side.

The smell was growing stronger with every passing moment, and as he pushed open the door with his nose Pommes Frites paused and sniffed appreciatively. The scent had now taken on a slightly different flavour. Along with the odour of bay rum, there were overtones of sweat and . . . yes, there was definitely more than a trace of fear. Instinct told Pommes Frites that he had the advantage of his prey.

Licking his lips in anticipation, he headed towards a flight of stairs immediately facing him.

Number 7-*bis* was old and rambling, and sadly in need of repair. High up on the outside wall overlooking the market an inscription recorded the fact that the Emperor Napoleon himself had once stayed there for lunch (from twelve fifteen until a quarter past two) during his long march across the Alps. But that had been a long time ago, on the 23rd June 1815. Since that happy day it had fallen into neglect, and had even escaped the attentions of the present progressive mayor—he of the 'CHIENS INTERDITS' sign, who was endeavouring to bring back to the town of St. Castille some of its former glories.

Pommes Frites had to pick his way very carefully up the ramshackle wooden staircase in order to avoid making any kind of noise; or even, for that matter, to avoid falling through it in some places.

On his way up he peered in at some empty rooms. In one there was a table with the remains of a meal, in another a couple of unmade camp beds. As he reached the third landing an ominous metallic click from somewhere close at hand caused him to stop in his tracks. He froze for a moment, then quickened his pace. Not for nothing had he attended a two-day seminar on ballistics; the only dog of his particular year to gain maximum marks and the coveted Golden Bone.

The sound meant only one thing. There was someone on the floor above with a gun, and if the heavy breathing was anything to go by, that some-one was in a hurry.

Covering the remaining stairs at something ap-proaching the speed of sound, Pommes Frites struck, and having struck, held on for all he was worth.

As he sank his teeth into the posterior of the figure on the far side of the room, a most satisfac-tory noise emerged from its other end; the first of a whole series of satisfactory noises.

It was an amalgamation which would have brought tears of joy to even the most fastidious of recording engineers in search of the esoteric in the way of sound effects. Not, perhaps, destined for the Top Ten, but assured of a place for ever more in the libraries of all self-respecting drama studios the world over.

Cataloguing would, of course, always present a problem, for it was hard to pin-point the dominant theme. Put at its simplest it was the cry of a man of Italian extraction, leaning out of a third-floor window in a small French town and taking aim at a distant target with a high-powered rifle. (Sounds of busy market nearby and hum of distant traffic in background.) Being attacked by fierce dog. Assorted barks and growls. Tearing of cloth. Cries of pain. Firing of rifle, followed by more cries of pain and alarm (mostly in Italian) as man falls from window and lands on second-floor balcony below. Sound of balcony giving way. More cries, some in It., but predominantly Fr. as man lands on barrow of fruit and veg. in street below. (12.5 secs.)

Pommes Frites stood with his paws on the windowsill and gazed down at the scene below. He felt slightly disappointed about the balcony. It hadn't entered into his calculations and it marred what might otherwise have been a perfect operation; one which he knew would have won the approval of his master.

Talking of which . . . looking up, he noticed a gap in the buildings opposite. Through it he had a clear view of the Square du Centre, La Langoustine, and—on the far side—a familiar figure standing outside the telephone booth. Even from that distance Monsieur Pamplemousse looked somewhat impatient.

It was time to go. Already he could hear footsteps and voices on the stairs. Being no fool Pommes Frites decided to avail himself of a second flight of stairs at the rear of the building.

A few minutes later he ambled into the square looking as if he hadn't a care in the world.

'Pommes Frites!' Monsieur Pamplemousse's voice held a touch of asperity. 'And where have you been?' He wagged his finger in mock reproof. 'The *boucherie, n'est-ce pas?*'

Pommes Frites gave a sigh. The *boucherie* indeed! Why was it that even the best and nicest of humans always suspected the worst. Really, there was no justice in the world. No justice at all.

He had half a mind not to give his master the present he'd brought him, but after a brief struggle his good nature and early training got the better of him. Reaching up, he dropped a small, shiny object into Monsieur Pamplemousse's outstretched hand.

It was cylindrical in shape, 7.5mm in diameter and despite its sojourn in Pommes Frites' mouth, still had the strong and unmistakable smell of cordite, a fact which did not go unnoticed or unrewarded by its recipient.

Pommes Frites wagged his tail as his master reached down to pat him. He couldn't have wished for a nicer reward.

6

WEDNESDAY EVENING

'*MERDE! SACREBLEU! NOM D'UN NOM!*' MONsieur Pamplemousse gazed in frustration at the unwrapped contents of a parcel which littered his bed. He was not in a good mood.

For a start, the journey to Orange and back had taken much longer than he'd anticipated. At any other time it would have been a pleasant way of passing an afternoon. First the drive through the great lavender-growing area of the Vaucluse; at this time of the year the plants already cropped and looking for all the world like row upon row of freshly barbered hedgehogs on parade and ready for inspection. Then the drop down through the Gorge de la Nesque via the D942 to the melon country of Carpentras, with the opportunity of making a short detour in order to sample the delights of a glass or two of the delicious sweet Beaumes de Venise. It would have been a good way of combining business with pleasure, for as well as commenting on food *Le Guide* also offered advice on the best and most enjoyable ways of getting from one restaurant to the next.

But things had not turned out as planned. The rot had set in at Orange itself with the discovery that the TGV high-speed train didn't stop there. Not only did it fail to stop, its specially laid track enabled it to ignore the city altogether and head straight for Avignon at a speed of something like 260 kilometres an hour.

Wondering what the Romans would have thought about this slight to a city they had helped to create and make beautiful, Monsieur Pamplemousse hurtled after the train in his 2CV, covering the first half of the thirty or so kilometres at a speed which would have caused M. André Citroën to gaze in wonder had he been alive and able to witness the event.

Unfortunately, wonderment was not one of the emotions shown by a gendarme when he came off the *autoroute* at Avignon Nord. The stern, implacable disapproval etched into his face left no room for other, finer feelings as he compared the entry time on Monsieur Pamplemousse's card with that indicated by his watch.

The practice of holding spot speed checks on the *autoroute* was something Monsieur Pamplemousse was aware of but had never actually encountered before, and he wished it could have happened at any other time.

Arguing was a waste of time. He went on his way eventually with a wallet which was considerably lighter than when he'd first set out, and reached the *gare* at Avignon long after the train had arrived and gone on its way again. That, in turn, meant his parcel received rather more attention than he would have liked.

The discretion in the filing system about which *Poupées Fantastiques* had boasted obviously did not extend to their labelling department. Either that or Oscar had deliberately tried to get his own back, for he'd seldom seen quite such a blatant advertisement on the outside of a package. An over-zealous official behind the counter refused delivery until it had been opened and its contents put on display for all to see. Trying to brazen things out by pulling his old rank had been a mistake too. The man had called his bluff.

The whole affair had been so upsetting he'd lost his way taking a short cut somewhere up in the mountains on the return journey and both he and Pommes Frites had arrived at La Langoustine tired, late and hungry.

Pommes Frites had been no help whatsoever. Normally Pommes Frites liked car rides. He enjoyed nothing better than bowling along with his master at the wheel and the side window open so that he could poke his head out from time to time and feel the cool breeze on his face and whiskers.

But today was an exception. He was still feeling the effects of the previous night's encounters. A certain stiffness had set in, a stiffness which hadn't been helped by all the exercise that morning. In short, Pommes Frites would much sooner have stayed where he was, recovering. However, he hadn't been given any choice in the matter. Without so much as a by-your-leave, he'd been bundled into the car and had had to endure over 340 kilometres of winding roads—more if you counted the extra kilometres they'd travelled trying to find the right one back, and it had put him into one of his difficult moods. Having refused to wear his seat belt, he kept leaning against Monsieur Pamplemousse every time they went round a right-hand bend, and threatening to burst open the offside door every time they rolled in the opposite direction. In the end Monsieur Pamplemousse put his foot down metaphorically as well as in practice and banished Pommes Frites to the back seat, an indignity he suffered in silence until just before St. Castille, when he'd been sick.

The only consolation to show for the afternoon—and Monsieur Pamplemousse was man enough to admit it—lay in the fact that the model itself, seen in all its inflated glory, was a masterpiece of the *poupée* maker's art. A symphony in wood and rubber. His warning must have gone home—for an unknown hand had even gone to the trouble of turning it into a rough likeness of himself with the addition of a moustache. An optional extra which made even Pommes Frites look twice. Perhaps—who knows?—it might have been someone he'd come up against in the old days and done a good turn for. Whatever the reason, ten out of ten for initiative.

It had been a strange experience, blowing it up with the aid of Pommes Frites' gas cylinder and seeing it grow into his own shape before his very eyes. Pommes Frites had been most surprised—seeing an effigy of his master instead of the usual kennel. It wasn't at all what he'd expected and he spent some time sniffing the result and wondering what on earth was going to happen.

Where they had managed to get the wooden legs from at such short notice, Monsieur Pamplemousse neither knew nor cared. It was sufficient that the job had been done to his satisfaction. Although it wouldn't have fooled anyone in the cold light of day, at night—with the lights turned out—who knew? It was worth a go.

He found his pyjama jacket and put it on over the top half, smiling to himself as he pulled back the bed cover. In one respect at least, *Poupées Fantastiques* had done him a great compliment. Madame Sophie, when she returned that night, would certainly have nothing to complain about—provided the electric mechanism stood up to the strain.

Making some final adjustments to the position of the model, he inserted one end of a long lead into a socket at the base of the spine—the one which according to figure fifteen in the instruction manual connected to the pressure-operated *membre*, and ran it carefully up the bed and over the end of the mattress, passing it underneath to a point about halfway down, where he looped it round one of the bedsprings for good measure.

It was as he paused to consult the instruction manual again before connecting the free end to a large battery box that his jaw suddenly dropped. The battery box, said the manual, in the casual terms reserved for such matters, will require eight 1.5 volt rechargeable batteries. He searched through the wrapping paper. They had not been included.

'*Imbéciles!*' Where was he to get eight 1.5 volt batteries in St. Castille at this time of night? It would be bad enough trying to get one battery. One battery he might be able to borrow from someone's torch, or two even—but eight—rechargeable ones at that!

For a moment or so he toyed with the idea of getting into his car again and going in search of a late-night garage. There must be one in the area. On the other hand . . . Monsieur Pamplemousse's knowledge of things electrical was not of the highest, but he did know that a car battery contained considerably more power in just one of its cells than a whole drawerful of torch batteries. He well remembered having once seen a car go up in flames because of a short-circuited battery; once they got going there was nothing to stop them. In the circumstances, a car battery might be an ideal power source for Madame Sophie's needs. If the worst came to the worst he could always get it recharged in the morning.

Some ten minutes later Monsieur Pamplemousse staggered up the back stairs carrying a large object wrapped in a car rug.

Shortly afterwards, having bared the ends of the lead, he twisted them round the two terminals, added some adhesive tape from his first-aid kit for good measure to make doubly sure they didn't come adrift in the heat of the moment, and pushed the battery under the bed.

Now for the big moment. The *moment critique*.

Closing the shutters in case he was being overlooked, he turned off all the lights except one and, under the watchful gaze of Pommes Frites, approached the figure on the bed.

Turning back the sheets, he gave the *membre* a tentative tweak. Almost immediately there was a click followed by a faint humming sound and things began to happen.

The result was beyond his wildest expectations. My word, but things had progressed since the old days. In the old days he'd heard tell of inflatable models being exported for the benefit of lonely guardians of what remained of the French colonial empire, but they had been of the opposite gender and certainly not—at least in his experience—readily available on the home market.

The whole thing was a miracle of ingenuity. Those areas which needed to contract, contracted. Those which needed to expand, grew large, gathering speed with every passing moment, vibrating in sympathy with the heaving buttocks, while the mouth opened and closed in random fashion emitting such lifelike moans and groans that even Pommes Frites' hackles began to rise.

Madame Sophie was in for a high old time that night. He wouldn't have minded being a fly on the pillow. If all went well she would be able to add her name to *Poupées Fantastiques'* list of satisfied customers in the truest sense of the word.

He consulted the instruction book again. There was no sense in wasting the battery. Besides, all the heaving and moaning was making him feel restive. Finding the right diagram at last he reached for the pressure-operated switch which controlled the vital organ. The humming died away.

He tried it several more times—just to make sure everything was working properly. It really was most intriguing. A tweak in one direction and the model relaxed with a hiss of escaping air. A tweak in the other and it started up again.

But if Monsieur Pamplemousse was fascinated by the gyrations of the figure on the bed, Pommes Frites was beside himself with excitement. He couldn't believe his eyes. Firmly convinced that it was some new kind of everlasting bone dispenser he began running around in circles, giving vent to growls of anticipation. He'd been given an everlasting bone once at Christmas and it had kept him going for several weeks; he couldn't wait to sink his teeth into it.

It was as the hubbub was at its height and he was nearing his fiftieth lap of the bedroom, barking his head off with delight, that he suddenly skidded to a halt and stared at the door. Or rather, he stared at the spot where the door had been the previous time round. Now it was open.

'Monster! . . . Pervert! . . . Unhappy man!'

Monsieur Pamplemousse jumped to his feet, but it was too late for explanations, if indeed he could readily have thought of one. Before he had a chance to open his mouth the door closed and the chambermaid disappeared, but not before she had ostentatiously removed the requirement notice from the handle and placed it outside. As far as she was concerned the room could stay *occupé* for all time. Such depravity was quite beyond belief. If she hadn't witnessed it with her own eyes she would not have thought such things were possible.

Feeling as deflated as the figure on the bed, Monsieur Pamplemousse gave the wiring a final check and then pulled the cover into place. All good things come to an end sooner or later and even Pommes Frites seemed somewhat sobered by the experience as he exchanged glances with his master.

Shortly afterwards, freshly bathed and with the dust of the journey removed, Monsieur Pamplemousse emerged from his room and with Pommes Frites leading the way headed down the stairs for a much needed dinner.

Madame Douard was busy at the reception desk with a late arrival. As he passed their eyes met briefly and he felt the colour rise to his cheeks. Madame Sophie had large eyes. Large and round, a strange mixture of innocence and promise. At the moment they were full of promise.

Monsieur Pamplemousse mopped his brow as he entered the dining room. *Mon Dieu!* If only he'd been thirty years younger. Alas, such opportunities had never come his way when he was eighteen; or perhaps they had and he'd been too shy to take advantage of them. Life could be very unsatisfactory at times.

On the other hand, only that very morning when he'd been out for a walk with Pommes Frites he'd caught sight of Madame Sophie disappearing into the local *bricolage*—no doubt to replenish her supply of sandpaper, probably with a coarser grade. Far better to devote his energies to safer things. He'd noted earlier in the day that *Loup* was on the menu; *Loup en Croûte Douard*—one of the patron's specialities. Perhaps he would indulge himself. *Soupe aux Moules Safranées* to begin with; the whole washed down with a Meursault—the '76. He felt his taste buds begin to throb; the kind of throbbing which could only be assuaged by a Kir Royale. One made with his favourite champagne: Gosset.

There was a thump, thump against his right leg as Pommes Frites wagged his tail with anticipation. Monsieur Pamplemousse was not the only one with active taste buds.

'Great minds discuss ideas, average minds discuss events, small minds discuss people. Me, I discuss none of these things. I am a chef and I talk of food.'

Monsieur Douard's booming laugh echoed round the deserted square. 'That is also why I do not wish to discuss Sophie. In her own way she is a good wife. She runs the hotel like a dream. Nothing escapes her eye. She looks after the money. The bills are always paid on time. The customers go on their way happy, and she leaves me alone to get on with my work. What more could a man wish for?'

Monsieur Pamplemousse was tempted to say a wife who didn't jump into bed with the clients at the drop of a hat, but Auguste forestalled him.

'If she has her little peccadilloes on the side, that is her affair. It does no great harm.'

Thinking of his aching muscles, Monsieur Pamplemousse came to the conclusion that harm, like most things in life, was only relative. All the same, picturing what was safely tucked in his bed upstairs, he couldn't help but wish the conversation would take another turn. Monsieur Douard was obviously trying to tell him something he would really rather not know about. Worse still, it was getting late and it would be an even greater embarrassment if, on his way to bed, Auguste met Sophie en route to her assignation.

'The great sadness of life,' he said, trying to change the subject, 'is our ignorance when young that first love can ever end.'

'My friend,' Monsieur Douard was obviously reading his thoughts with uncanny accuracy. 'Do not distress yourself. To tell you the truth, I am grateful. When one is at work all day in a hot kitchen there is little time left over to take care of other things.'

Monsieur Pamplemousse forebore to comment that in his travels he'd met a good many chefs who found their appetites more than whetted by the time they'd spent in their kitchen. Hotted up, in fact. In life, if you really wanted something you made time for it.

'Most mornings,' continued Monsieur Douard, 'I am up at five. I have to go to the market to make sure I get fresh vegetables. I have to go to the butcher to make certain the meat is as I wish it to be. Then I have to see what fish is available so that I can come back and prepare the menu. Then there are many people to see; the *négociant* about the wine; people who have been supplying me with cheese over the years—small farmers from up in the mountains, representatives from the big suppliers; people I know who grow fruit for me specially and who bring it when it is exactly right for picking, not a day too early and not a day too late.

'Then, and only then, can I really begin work. At the end of the day it is nourishment I require—not punishment. It has always been that way—ever since we were first married. Sophie understands my feelings and I respect hers. She is a woman with an abundance of love—some might say an over-abundance, and she loves to give. It is her nature.

'Over the years there have been many. In the beginning the *sous-chef* had to go. He was never at his post. Then there was the *garde-manger,* guests, the *facteur* . . . in their time they have all drunk their fill, including the odd-job man. *Especially* the odd-job man. She has a strange proclivity for wood.

107

She should have been in a circus. Give her the smell of sawdust and she is away. There is no stopping her. There are things I could tell you . . .'

Monsieur Pamplemousse rather hoped he wouldn't. He felt doubly glad he'd placed his order with *Poupées Fantastiques*. He hoped it would stand the strain.

But Auguste was warming to his subject. He waved towards the statue in the middle of the square. 'She is a true descendant of Hortense and no mistake.'

Monsieur Pamplemousse followed his gaze. Whoever had sculptured Hortense had been fortunate enough to capture her in what could only be termed an unguarded moment. Bending over in order to pick some flowers, on what was presumably a summer's day, for she was totally unclothed, the pose had afforded ample opportunity to highlight what were undoubtedly her best features, her *derrière* and *doudounnes* enhanced still more by the forces of gravity. In the moonlight, and seen from a certain angle, Monsieur Pamplemousse had to agree that the figure bore a striking resemblance to Madame Sophie, although he was too much of a gentleman to say so.

Monsieur Douard broke across his thoughts. 'She is very beautiful, that one. The story goes that she is under a spell . . . that she is waiting . . . has been waiting all these years for someone to come and . . . release her. Someone, that is . . . who understands.

'Poof! It is all nonsense, of course. But there are some things—like Papa Nöel—in which it is nice to believe.' He gave a nudge. 'Perhaps it is the same with Sophie. Perhaps she, too, is waiting. She will not have long, *n'est-ce pas?*'

Monsieur Pamplemousse gave a nervous laugh. In spite of himself his voice sounded cracked and dry. He licked his lips and downed the last of the Armagnac.

'Another?'

He shook his head. 'No, thank you. Pommes Frites and I may take a stroll before we retire.'

Monsieur Douard stood up and held out his hand. 'In that case, my friend, forgive me if I don't join you. I have to be up early. Enjoy yourselves. It is a beautiful night.'

As Auguste disappeared into the hotel a figure rose into view from beneath a nearby table, stretched, and then joined Monsieur Pamplemousse at the top of the steps leading down from the terrace.

Together they set out across the square. Monsieur Pamplemousse paused by the fountain and glanced up. Douard had been right. Hortense *was* beautiful. Deliciously, delightfully, provocatively beautiful. Surveying the world through half-closed eyes, her lips were parted slightly as if she was about to be kissed. Better still, as if she wanted to be kissed. She appeared to be staring straight at him, and there was about her an air of voluptuous, ill-concealed abandon, which caused strange stirrings inside his stomach.

At that moment a car came round the corner of the square, its headlights picking out the statue momentarily as it shot past. For a brief moment Monsieur Pamplemousse had a feeling that one of Hortense's eyes had closed in a wink, then it was gone—a trick of the light.

He shook himself. It was totally and utterly ridiculous. Perhaps the Armagnac had been a mistake.

'Pommes Frites,' he said. 'You and I are going for a very *long* walk.'

Pommes Frites indulged his master with a wag of his tail. As far as he was concerned there was nothing stopping them. A statue was a statue was a statue. They were made of stone and having said that you'd more or less covered the subject. He'd already left his mark more than once on the side of the fountain belonging to this one, *and* slaked his thirst into the bargain. He saw no particular reason to linger any longer.

Somewhere not far away there was the sound of a car turning. From the way the engine was being revved the driver was obviously in a great hurry. Probably a late-night traveller who'd taken the wrong turning and was cursing his luck. It seemed to be heading back the way it had come. There was a squeal of tyres as it rounded a corner and entered the square.

Expecting it to follow the normal line of traffic anti-clock-wise round the statue, Monsieur Pamplemousse was about to move out of its way round the other side when some sixth sense signalled an urgent warning. Shouting to Pommes Frites to get out of the way, he made a leap for the safety of the fountain. Jumping on to the edge he was propelled forward by his own momentum and only saved himself from falling into the water by clutching the back of Hortense.

He felt the draught from the car as it hurtled past, its driver clutching the wheel while two white faces peered out at him from the back window. It was the same car that had followed him up into the hills the day he'd met Giampiero.

Looking round, he breathed a sigh of relief. Pommes Frites had managed to scramble clear as well.

Glancing over his shoulder he could see the lights of the car as it disappeared up the hill the way it had come. Pushing against Hortense's shoulders he inched his way slowly downwards until he was clasping her bottom. After a pause for breath he gave a heave. As he did so he felt a faint rocking movement. *Quelle horreur!* He would never be able to show his face in St. Castille again if he pushed the statue off its perch and Madame Hortense broke in two. He held his breath and tried again. There was an ominous creak from somewhere below.

Very slowly he turned his head and caught sight of Pommes Frites standing some distance away staring at him; or rather staring, he realised, at something a little way beyond him.

Equally slowly he turned his head back the other way and then suppressed a groan as he saw a familiar figure watching him.

'Testing the legend, I see. How very romantic.'

Monsieur Pamplemousse glared at the speaker. Inspector Banyuls seemed to have perfected an uncanny knack of appearing at the least opportune moment. He must spend most of his waking hours lying in wait.

'*Péquenot!*' he muttered under his breath. There was no other word for it. That was what he was ... *un péquenot*. A hick. He wouldn't last two minutes in somewhere like Paris.

Taking the bull by the horns, he pushed against

111

Madame Hortense with all his might. Better a broken statue than suffer the indignity of Banyuls' stares a moment longer than was necessary. As he toppled backwards he was mortified to feel a helping hand reach out in the nick of time to prevent him falling back into the road.

Regaining his balance he jumped to the ground and glared at the inspector as he brushed himself down.

'Instead of just standing idly by,' he growled, 'you would be better employed in the pursuit of the car that forced me up there in the first place.'

'Car? What car? I saw no car.'

Monsieur Pamplemousse glared at him. 'If you won't go after it,' he bellowed, 'then I will.'

Signalling to Pommes Frites, he strode across the square to where his own car was parked, climbed in, slammed the door and pressed the starter.

In the silence that followed he felt rather than saw a shadow loom up against the side window. There was a tap, then the door opened.

'Well?' said Inspector Banyuls sarcastically. 'Don't tell me you have changed your mind.'

'Someone,' said Monsieur Pamplemousse with as much dignity as he could muster, 'seems to have taken my battery.'

'What!' A sudden change came over Inspector Banyuls. He reached inside his pocket and took out a note-book. 'This is serious.'

Monsieur Pamplemousse gazed at him. How could anyone be such an oaf as to ignore what he was convinced amounted to yet another attempt on his life and yet spring into action on hearing about a missing battery? He'd been nearly poisoned, shot at, had his balcony railings sawn through, escaped death by inches from a maniac in a car . . . words failed him. The man's mind was an arid desert.

'I will give you a clue,' he said slowly and distinctly. 'It is my belief that the person who took it is not a million miles from this very spot, and if you meet him I should treat him with the greatest respect. He is undoubtedly highly dangerous and may well render you grievous bodily harm.'

Deriving what little satisfaction he could from the parting shot, he climbed out of the car again and with Pommes Frites at his heels set off briskly towards the Grande Avenue Charles de Gaulle. Pommes Frites had long since given up trying to follow what was going on. He was wearing his mournful expression, the one he kept for occasions when things promised—like after-dinner walks—took a long time to materialise.

Monsieur Pamplemousse felt he could delay matters no longer.

It was late when they got back. Pommes Frites had been determined to get his pound of flesh. The clock over the Hôtel de Ville already showed past midnight, and by the time Monsieur Pamplemousse had inflated the new kennel and said good night the half hour had also struck.

Finding the rear entrance locked, he made his way round to the front of the hotel and with a nod to the gendarme who was still on duty just inside the doorway, crossed the hall to the stairs.

Halfway up he thought he heard a muffled explosion coming from one of the floors above. He sniffed. There was a smell of burning coming from somewhere not too far away. Rubbery, rather like a

vacuum cleaner which is about to give up the
ghost. That was all that was needed to round off
the evening—a fire!

Hurrying up the remaining few stairs he was
about to turn on to the landing when instinct told
him to slow down. Luck was with him. Peering
round the corner he was just in time to see Madame Sophie leaving his room. She was, to say the
least, in a state of *déshabillé*. Her hair hung about
her shoulders in ringlets, most of her front appeared
to be covered by some kind of black deposit, and
from the brief glimpse he had of her face it wore a
glazed expression like that of a believer who has
just been awarded the honour of the last waltz
with her favourite guru. Oblivious to all about her,
she turned and groped her way along the corridor,
finally disappearing into her quarters at the far end
like someone in a trance.

As soon as the coast was clear Monsieur Pamplemousse hurried after her. As he drew near his door
the source of the smoke was only too clear. Wafts
of it were emerging from the gap at the bottom.
Holding a handkerchief over his nose he pushed it
open and went inside. It was even worse than he
had expected. It smelt and looked like a charnel
house.

Gasping for breath he crossed to the shutters
and flung them open, then turned, prepared for
the worst.

His bed was a sorry sight. Rumpled sheets were
one thing, and in the circumstances not unexpected, but of the *poupée*, apart from the two
wooden legs and a motley collection of wires, rods
and sundry items of unidentifiable electronic de-
vices, little remained but a smouldering heap

of blackened rubber. Like the rim of an all too active volcano, they surrounded a large hole in the centre of the mattress.

Through it he could see the twisted remains of his car battery. Placing it immediately below the bedsprings had obviously been a cardinal error. He'd taken no account of Madame Sophie's weight, nor her enthusiasm once she got going. She must have cut through the wire and caused a short circuit. If Banyuls knew what had really happened to the battery he would have filled his note-book a dozen times over. How he would ever face the chambermaid again he didn't know.

While he was thinking the matter over, Monsieur Pamplemousse heard a slight sound at the door. He turned and saw a sheet of notepaper lying on the carpet. It had a familiar look.

The words confirmed his worst fears.

'Dearest one of the darkness,' he read. 'You who remain so silent and yet have so much to give. When I left you tonight you seemed strangely deflated, and yet . . . and yet, each time we meet . . . is it only twice? . . . each time is more exquisite than the one before. I thought I knew you, but tonight was different again. What will tomorrow bring? I cannot wait . . . although I know I have to. Until then . . . your loving S.'

Merde! Monsieur Pamplemousse sat down on the end of the bed and buried his head in his hands. Now he was really *dans le chocolat*. A dying sizzle came from somewhere underneath, but he ignored it. It was no good. Tomorrow he would have to go through the whole rigmarole again. What next? Perhaps . . . perhaps the Mark V—the one with the optional extras—whatever they might be.

He opened his suitcase and reached inside for the catalogue which had been enclosed with the parcel from *Poupées Fantastiques*. Sleep would not come as easily as usual that night.

7

THURSDAY AFTERNOON

AT FOURTEEN HUNDRED HOURS PRECISELY on the following day, Monsieur Pamplemousse, replete from a most satisfactory *déjeuner* at the Bar du Centre, picked up his receipted bill and set off across the square towards his hotel.

He felt at peace with the world. The word *cuisine* had many meanings and variations, but in his humble opinion one of its most rewarding peaks lay within a freshly baked *baguette*, split down the middle, lightly buttered, with perhaps a dash of *Moutarde de Dijon* to taste, and then filled with slices of ham—preferably from the Ardennes and tasting of the smoke from the trees of the forest and the maize and acorn diet on which the pigs had been reared. When it was washed down with a bottle of local wine, such as the Chateau Vignelaure he'd been privileged to drink that day, there was nothing finer.

It was a view with which Pommes Frites heartily

117

concurred. Apart, that is, from the mustard. Pommes Frites didn't like mustard. It made his eyes water.

Monsieur Pamplemousse made a metal note to confirm the Bar du Centre's entry in *Le Guide*. Not with a Stock Pot—they would neither expect it nor thank him for it, but certainly with a wrought iron table and chair—the symbol which denoted a good place to stop en route, and a cut above the award of a mere bar stool.

One way and another it had been a busy morning. There had been the ordering of a new *poupée*—the Mark V this time complete with batteries, to be sent direct to the hotel without delay. That in itself had taken a great deal of argument and had used up most of his small change. Oscar had not been keen on the idea at all. In the end he'd had to resort to threats again, but it had left him feeling weary. Arguments always did.

Then he'd had to change his car battery. The plates on the old one were buckled beyond hope. That had taken most of the morning. The Citroën agent was at the other end of town, too far to carry the old one. And when he'd finally got it there on the back of a borrowed bicycle he'd encountered a distinct lack of enthusiasm about taking it in part exchange.

Halfway across the square he heard someone call out his name and turned to see Giampiero hurrying towards him. He looked worried.

'Is it true about last night?'

Monsieur Pamplemousse stifled a sigh. The chambermaid must have been talking. Not that he could blame her—she probably couldn't wait.

'I heard the car going past from my room. I

rushed to the end of the corridor but by then it was too late. I saw you and Inspector Banyuls by the fountain, so I guessed you were all right. Then, soon after, I heard a bang . . . it sounded as though it came from the direction of your room. After that I smelt smoke . . .'

Monsieur Pamplemousse hesitated, wondering whether to tell the full story, then thought better of it. 'It wouldn't be the first time someone has tried to do away with me.'

'Perhaps.' It was Giampiero's turn to hesitate, then he, too, seemed to change his mind. 'But take care.' He held out his hand. 'It is possible we may be leaving soon. Eva is getting restive. She wishes to move on.' Again there was a slight hesitation.

'I'm sorry.' Really there was little more to be said. In any case he was anxious to be on his way. It was kind of Giampiero to bother about his well-being and although it was true that it wouldn't be the first time someone had been out to do him harm, that was long ago. He felt more than able to take care of himself. Besides, it was nearly five past the hour.

Entering the garden behind La Langoustine by a side gate, he made his way towards a small hexagonal iron and glass gazebo standing in the centre of a small patch of rough grass which served as a lawn. He was pleased to see that it was still empty.

As he sat down a waiter emerged from the rear of the hotel carrying a silver tray on which reposed a silver pot filled with coffee, a cup and saucer, and a large balloon-shaped glass containing Armagnac.

Having placed it on the table in the centre of the gazebo and made sure that all was well, he retired gracefully from the scene, nursing the forlorn hope that the other occupants of the hotel might emulate Monsieur Pamplemousse and take their after-lunch drinks on the terrace, in the garden, or even—sparing Monsieur Pamplemousse—in the gazebo itself. Anywhere, so long as he could get on with clearing the tables. The waiters from La Langoustine were playing netball against a team from an hotel in the next village that afternoon and time was of the essence.

At fourteen-o-eight, Pommes Frites, having decided that there was nothing to be gained from hanging about, wandered off for a post-prandial nap, leaving his master to cogitate on life in general and the aftertaste of sandwiches *au jambon* and Armagnac in particular. It was hot in the gazebo and if he was going to have a nap he preferred to do it in the comfort of his kennel.

Monsieur Pamplemousse looked forward to his half hour or so of peace and quiet every afternoon. The gazebo was a new addition—so new it still had the steel ring on top which had been used to lift it into place—but it was ideal. It was amazing how quickly one settled down to a new routine. A few days in a place and it began to feel as though you had always lived there.

He would have been somewhat put out had he been able to read the waiter's mind. Fond of company when the occasion demanded, Monsieur Pamplemousse also placed great store on moments when he could be alone with his thoughts, which was quite a different matter to being lonely. Loneliness was often being by oneself in a crowd. Being alone of one's own choice was in its way a great luxury, so when he saw the girl from reception heading his way he pursed his lips with annoyance. From the agitated way she was behaving he could tell she was not the bearer of good news.

'A telephone call, Monsieur . . . from Paris.'

Monsieur Pamplemousse grunted. Who could it be, telephoning him in his lunch hour? 'Did they not give their name?'

'No, Monsieur. It was a man. He said it was urgent.'

'I will take it in my room.' Downing his Armagnac at a gulp, Monsieur Pamplemousse clambered to his feet and followed the girl back into the hotel.

At fourteen fifteen precisely, while he was making his way up to his room—a moment marked by the striking of the clock over the Hôtel de Ville—Albert, a *clochard* whose abode was rarely fixed and then usually at the whim of Inspector Banyuls or one of his subordinates, polished off the remains of a litre of a *vin* whose ordinariness needed to be tasted to be believed. Climbing unsteadily to his feet, he smacked his lips, which he then wiped on the sleeve of his tattered raincoat, crossed the street, and made towards the *chemiserie* of Madame Peigné, which was about to open for business.

Standing outside he opened his raincoat wide, thus exposing himself to Madame Peigné, who was about to unlock the door, and proceeded to go about his own business by the simple expedient of relieving himself on the glass panel.

Madame Peigné, who'd only had her windows

cleaned that very morning, gazed at the sight open-mouthed. Registering the fact, without being totally aware of it, that there was something very odd about Albert's anatomy, she uttered a short prayer and reached for the telephone on her counter.

Having many times rehearsed how to call for help in the dark in the event of an emergency, she was able to dial the correct number without missing a single moment of Albert's performance. She had read of such things. She had—let it be said—even dreamed of such things, although not nearly as often as she would have liked, but never had she expected to see what she was seeing in the flesh as it were. Albeit, and thankfully, it was separated from her by a sheet of plate glass—but there it was, as large as life if not twice as beautiful. Her feeling of relief that she hadn't actually got as far as unlocking the door was only outweighed by her desire to make the most of the situation. It was better than anything she had ever seen on television.

Inspector Banyuls tried to keep a straight voice. 'He is doing *what* with it?' he asked.

Madame Peigné gulped. 'He is brandishing it at me. And . . . and . . .'

'And *what*?' Inspector Banyuls tried not to sound too impatient.

'He . . . he has a balloon tied to the . . . the end of it. A large, red balloon.'

'May I have a description?'

'You mean . . . for the identification parade?' The voice at the other end could barely suppress its excitement. 'One moment while I get my glasses.'

Having posed the question, Inspector Banyuls

immediately regretted it. His words had obviously been misinterpreted. He put the receiver down, signalled to one of his subordinates, and made one of his very rare jokes.

'It seems,' he said with a thin smile, 'that St. Castille is *en fête*. Please go at once to Madame Peigné in the Rue Vaugarde. She is having trouble with the decorations.'

It was the last joke he was to make that day. He'd barely put the telephone down when it rang again.

This time it was Monsieur Dupré, outfitter, clothier, and senior partner in the firm of Dupré et fils, an establishment almost as ancient as La Langoustine itself, and whose windows had suffered—were still suffering if the occasional sound of breaking glass was anything to go by—indignities of an even more basic and destructive nature than those of the previous complainant.

'A brick?' repeated Inspector Banyuls. He glanced at his watch and entered the time—fourteen eighteen—on a pad in front of him. 'What sort of brick?'

His question unleashed a veritable torrent of abuse. A torrent which made it difficult to sort out the wheat of plain, unadorned truth from the chaff of uncontrolled indignation.

It seemed that Monsieur Dupré had been enjoying his usual leisurely lunch on the pavement outside the Bar du Centre on the other side of the square—a *steak frites* with salad, followed by a *crème caramel*—when, before his very eyes, a miscreant of the worst possible kind had struck, not once, but several times, leaving a hole in the window large enough to climb through.

'*Déshonorant! Scandaleux! Action sans intermé-*

diaire!' were just a few of the phrases Monsieur Dupré barked with matching gestures down the telephone at the back of the bar, while at the same time keeping a watchful eye on the goings on in his shop window across the square.

The *lourdaud* was even now trying on a pair of shoes—several sizes too small by the way he was mincing up and down. The backs would be broken for certain.

'Yes, yes, I will send someone round as soon as possible.' Inspector Banyuls' voice sounded wearily over the line. 'No, I cannot come myself. I cannot be in two places at once and I am needed here. There are many things happening at the moment and my forces are depleted.'

'I warn you, Banyuls, I am not without friends in the higher echelons.' Monsieur Dupré, his face growing redder and redder, gripped the telephone receiver rather as he might have gripped the throat of the transgressor on the other side of the square had he possessed the necessary courage. Even as he did so there was a click. He gazed at it disbelievingly for a moment. The impossible had happened. Banyuls had hung up on him.

There was another crash of breaking glass. Monsieur Dupré's uninvited guest was enjoying himself. It wasn't often one could break the law and be paid for doing it. Never one to question good fortune when it came his way—the Lord alone knew how rarely *that* was—he had accepted with alacrity a fat fee and the promise of free transport out of town at fourteen thirty-five hours if all went according to plan. No doubt in the fullness of time the law would catch up on him, but in the meantime he had a new jacket, a pocketful of socks, several ties and handkerchiefs, and a new pair of shoes. Sadly, two left-fitting ones, for Monsieur Dupré was not one to take chances and never left complete pairs on display in his window. But beggars could not be choosers; the trousers went very well with the jacket, and the shirt couldn't have been a better fit. As for the tie—he looked at his reflection in the mirror. It was many years since he'd last sported a tie.

Covering his arm for protection with another jacket, he enlarged the hole in the window and clambered out. The few passers-by who had stopped to watch, tempered their outrage by their very active dislike of Monsieur Dupré, who had grown fat and rich at their expense over the years. Reaching inside the window for a hat as a last-minute embellishment, the intruder waved goodbye to his audience and set off out of town towards his rendez-vous. It was now twenty-two minutes past the hour by the clock across the square and he would have to hurry.

In his office at the Commissariat de Police, Inspector Banyuls also checked the time, registered the fact in his mind that the *autobus* from Forcalquier had just passed his window on schedule, and reached for the telephone as it began to ring again.

What would it be this time? He couldn't remember ever having had a day like it before. Apart from the matters he had dealt with personally, reports were coming in of other strange happenings in various quarters of the town. No part of St. Castille was without its problems. There was the mysterious affair of the old crone with six—or was it seven?—children, all of whom had decided to squat in the middle of the main road to Digne and were refusing to budge. They had better be moved before the *autobus* went on its way or there would be hell to pay. Already he could hear the sound of irate car horns.

Then there was the case of old Madame Ranglaret. She'd emptied an entire bucket of slops over some American tourists who'd been taking a stroll round the old part of the town and had had the misfortune to pass under her window at the time. In fact, not just one bucket, but, according to all accounts, three! One bucket might have been an accident—but three! Where she'd got them all from goodness only knew. Madame Ranglaret had probably never owned more than one bucket in the whole of her life.

As for Dupré. He regretted hanging up on him. He would have to make amends in some way. On reflection, he, Banyuls, would deal with the matter personally. Not for nothing had Monsieur Dupré contributed to the police funds over the years.

It was going to involve a lot of paperwork. As if he didn't have enough on his plate already.

He picked up the receiver. 'Banyuls here.'

But if Inspector Banyuls hoped for some kind of respite from his problems he was unlucky. As the voice at the other end spluttered forth its indignation he reached for a pad.

'One moment . . . let me get that down. You say you are playing *boules* against a team from Digne . . . their *pointeur* had just committed a *pousse-pousse*.'

Inspector Banyuls was no *boules* player, but he knew enough about the game to appreciate that in some circles, the very serious circles—and St.

Castille was in line to win the area championship, bowling a *pousse-pousse*—the act of making your ball end up as close to the *cochonnet* as possible and at the same time intentionally knocking your opponent's ball out of the way—was considered *de trop*.

He could picture the scene in the Square du Centre; the strip of gravel under the plane trees behind the fountain; the group of elderly citizens with their berets, their Gauloises, and their own personal locker against the wall; perhaps a sprinkling of younger bloods privileged to join in; the click of the balls and the grunts and imprecations and arguments as the play went first one way and then another. They were all probably too engrossed in the game to even notice the outrage being perpetrated in Monsieur Dupré's shop. Some, no doubt, were already looking forward to the traditional *pan bagna* after it was all over.

Placing his other hand over the receiver, he raised his eyebrows for the benefit of anyone who happened to be passing, and then realised that he was alone in the station. He must concentrate. It wasn't easy, for his caller was more than a trifle incoherent.

'Yes, yes, I understand. Your *tireur* was about to throw a *carreau*.' He gave a sigh. Why was it that in all walks of life a certain mumbo-jumbo had to be created in order to add to the mystique? Why couldn't the man simply say that the best thrower in the team was about to hurl his ball and try to knock his opponent's one for six, leaving his own in its place? It would be much simpler.

'Yes, I *do* know that Jean can crack a walnut at twenty paces, but I really do not see . . .' It was hard to tell where the conversation was leading.

Boules was undoubtedly an important matter, but . . .

'What? You have lost your *cochonnet*? Do you mean to say you have been talking to me all this time about a lost ball? Really . . .

'*What?*' Inspector Banyuls jumped to his feet. 'Would you mind repeating that? A man came out from the crowd of sightseers, picked up the *cochonnet* and did what with it? . . . He placed it in the letter box outside the P.T.T? The *Autres Régions* section? . . . Yes, yes, I know the P.T.T. does not reopen until fifteen hundred hours. I will be with you immediately.'

Slamming the receiver down, Inspector Banyuls reached for his belt and revolver.

Forces were at work in St. Castille which for the moment were beyond his understanding. There was a feeling of near anarchy in the air. But he would get to the bottom of it.

It was an unprecedented situation. Such a thing had never happened before. Not in his memory. The entire police force of the town was fully occupied. For the first time in its history he was going to have to lock up the station and leave it unattended.

Noting the time on his pad—fourteen twenty-three—he turned the key in the station door and made his way quickly towards the square. If he wasn't careful there could be a lynching. Already a large crowd had collected.

Ahead of him, the *autobus* had disgorged its passengers and was making ready to leave again. Reluctantly, for the driver was craning his neck to see what was going on. A solitary female figure in a fur coat was just disappearing with some luggage into the Hôtel Langoustine. From behind the hotel there were sounds of activity—a crane was moving into position, its jib turning and the giant grappling hook swinging through the air as it set to work. Close by a lorry was backing through a gap in the wall, revving its engine impatiently.

In his room on the first floor of the hotel Monsieur Pamplemousse was taking his call.

'. . . sorry to trouble you, Aristide. I wouldn't normally have telephoned, but we only got the news this morning. It is terrible. Terrible.'

'What news?' For a moment Monsieur Pamplemousse couldn't think what the other was talking about. Then he remembered. Time flew.

'Oh, it wasn't so bad. A bit of a shock at first. It was unexpected. It isn't every day one finds a head on one's plate. However, it's kind of you to ring.'

'A head?' It was the turn of the voice at the other end to sound puzzled. 'What head? I was telephoning about your accident. It is terrible news. Terrible. Both legs, I hear. The boys are arranging a collection.'

Monsieur Pamplemousse suppressed a groan. He wished he'd never thought of the idea. It seemed as though he would be plagued with it for the rest of his life; all for the sake of a momentary act of goodwill.

'They can't!' he exclaimed. 'They *mustn't*.'

'Nonsense! It's the least we can do.'

'But it isn't like that.' Monsieur Pamplemousse hovered between telling the truth with the risk of revealing all and embroidering his tale still further. If rumours could fly one way they could certainly fly the other. Perhaps a transplant? It was amazing what they could do these days. He would be able

129

to return to Paris a new man. But *two* legs, and from whom? Two different ones? Perhaps one male and one female? Or even two female? Now, *there* was fuel for thought ... A voice in his ear reminded him that the other was still speaking.

'There is talk of applying for a wheelchair through the Ministry. With your background ...'

'Look,' he broke in, 'I am saying there is no truth in the story—no truth whatsoever. But for the moment, while I am still here in St. Castille, I would rather it wasn't spoken about. I will explain it all when I get back to base.'

'No truth?' The voice at the other end sounded almost disappointed.

'I swear on my copy of *Le Guide*. The two legs I am standing on at this moment are not only flesh and blood, they are my own, as they always have been. As for the collection—you must give the money back at once. All of it. It would be most embarrassing ...'

'Oh, that's O.K. No trouble there. You know how it is ... the end of the month ... most people out on the road ... the Directeur always in conference. To tell you the truth, we haven't actually got very much yet. Everyone sends their felicitations, of course. The thing is ...'

'Well?' Monsieur Pamplemousse tried not to sound aggrieved.

'That's the other reason I'm phoning. To warn you ...'

'Warn me?'

'I wouldn't be in your shoes right now, that's for sure. Hey, can you stand a shock?' Monsieur Pamplemousse could have sworn the voice at the other end was about to break into a chuckle. He glanced at his watch impatiently. It was almost half past two. His coffee would be stone cold.

'Speak up, do.' He could hardly hear for the noise outside. The builders must be back at work earlier than usual. Apart from the rattle of the crane there was an infernal roar from one of the lorries. Above it all he suddenly heard a long drawn out howl from Pommes Frites.

'One moment.' Holding the receiver at arm's length he crossed to the balcony. As he reached out to pull the shutters closed he glanced down into the courtyard below. Pommes Frites appeared to be struggling to free himself from his kennel. For some reason or other—perhaps a nightmare following his lunch—he must have stood up too quickly. He looked for all the world like an arctic explorer dressed in one of those bulbous waterproof jackets that were all the rage. As he watched, Pommes Frites managed to struggle free at last and ran barking across the garden, peering upwards as he did so.

Monsieur Pamplemousse followed his gaze and suddenly became transfixed at the sight which met his eyes.

There, not a stone's throw away, rising inexorably into the air on the end of the crane's cable, was the gazebo. The very same gazebo in which he'd been sitting only moments before. The hook on the end of the cable had been slipped through the steel ring which surmounted it. Miraculously his coffee things and the empty Armagnac glass were still in place on the table.

But it wasn't any of these trivial details or the mournful sound of Pommes Frites' howls that caused him to blanch; it was the sight of a solitary white-faced occupant, clutching a parasol with one hand and the side of the gazebo with the other as it swung in a circular motion while the crane shunted back on its rails.

Before he had a chance to call out, the jib moved away from the window. The movement sent the hut spinning, as with more haste than finesse it began lowering it on the other side of the garden wall.

'Hullo! Hullo!' A series of whistling noises brought Monsieur Pamplemousse back to earth again with the realisation that he was still holding the telephone receiver. He held it up to his ear.

'Ah, there you are. What on earth's going on? As I was saying, this may come as a bit of a shock, but you see . . . when your wife heard the news she left for St. Castille at once. There was nothing we could do to stop her. She should be with you any moment now. I thought I had better warn you . . .'

The rest of the words were lost as there came a roar of an engine. Monsieur Pamplemousse gripped the receiver in his clenched hand as he leaned out of the window across the balcony to see what was happening.

'Doucette has not only arrived,' he said grimly, 'she has already left again. She came past my window not ten seconds ago in a gazebo, and at this very moment she is on the back of a lorry speeding God knows where . . . Pommes Frites is about to set off in pursuit, but I fear the worst.'

They were the last words he was to utter for some while. Straining to the utmost in order to follow the progress of the lorry he made a grab for the rail and realised all too late that it was no longer there. He felt himself falling. Halfway down he remembered he'd moved Pommes Frites' kennel. Then everything went black.

8

FRIDAY MORNING

'I AM SORRY TO DISTURB YOU.' MONSIEUR Pamplemousse stirred and shook himself awake. Ever since his fall he'd been confoundedly sleepy, hardly able to keep his eyes open for more than a few seconds at a time. His mouth felt dry. He suspected drugs but had no recollection of being given any.

He sat up and gazed at Inspector Banyuls, poised at the side of the bed, note-book in hand.

'What time is it?'

'Eleven thirty in the morning.'

Monsieur Pamplemousse concentrated his thoughts. 'It can't be,' he said at last. 'I remember very clearly having lunch at the Bar du Centre . . .'

Inspector Banyuls allowed himself one of his rare smiles. 'That was yesterday—Thursday. Today is Friday. Friday morning. As I was saying, I do not wish to disturb you . . . for obvious reasons.' He nodded towards a large mound at the bottom of the bed. 'But if we are to have any success in our search we must have a description.'

'Friday?' Monsieur Pamplemousse looked instinctively for his watch. A lighter patch of flesh marked where it had been. He had a momentary feeling of panic, as if a lifeline had been cut off. Then, to his relief, he saw it on the table beside the bed. Alongside it was his favourite Cross pen. He reached for the watch, checked Banyuls' statement, and slipped it back on his wrist. Things were slowly swimming into place. The telephone call. The gazebo. Doucette . . . the broken balcony . . . Pommes Frites barking as he ran off in pursuit of the lorry . . .

'I repeat. We must have a description.'

'Of course . . . I understand. Let me see . . .' This was no good. No good at all. He must concentrate.

'Fairly large, I would say. Tall, that is . . . not in weight. The weight is about forty-five to fifty kilograms. Deeply sunk eyes—a mixture of hazel and yellow. Large ears. Looks rather sorrowful. The hair . . . the hair is a mixture of colours. Black and tan with a little red here and there, flecked with white on the chest . . .'

Inspector Banyuls carried on making notes for a moment or two. His writing was like his moustache; small, thin, precise and well cared for. When he finally caught up with his words and read through them he let out a whistle.

'*Morbleu!* She sounds *formidable*. No wonder you holiday alone. Tell me, how long have you been married?'

Monsieur Pamplemousse gazed at him pityingly. '*Married*? I am not talking of my wife. I am talking of Pommes Frites.'

Inspector Banyuls seemed to have some difficulty in swallowing. Tearing off the page, he screwed it up into a tight ball and tossed it into a wastebin.

'I am not,' he said at long last, 'I never have been, and I never will be interested in Pommes Frites. I have better things to do with my time than look for stray dogs. Besides, he ate my best clue.' He made it sound like a schoolboy complaining about a lost ball.

Monsieur Pamplemousse glared at him. 'And I,' he said, drawing himself up as high as he could in the circumstances, 'have better things to do with my time than talk to nincompoops. How dare you talk of Pommes Frites in that way! You are not fit to tread the same ground he walks on. If you were lost together in the Sahara desert you would not deserve a sip at his water bowl. The sad fact is that he would readily allow it whereas it wouldn't even cross your tiny mind to share yours with him. If he is not found and found quickly I shall hold you personally responsible. And if any harm comes to him in the meantime I would not care to be in your shoes.'

Monsieur Pamplemousse sank back into his pillow, exhausted by the effort of his outburst, and awaited a return barrage. But to his surprise, the reply when it came was unusually mild.

Inspector Banyuls snapped his note-book shut and fastened it carefully with an elastic band. 'I realise,' he said, 'that you are a little overwrought after your . . . experience, therefore I shall ignore those remarks. I will return later in the day when you are more amenable to conversation.'

He crossed to the door and then paused and

looked curiously at Monsieur Pamplemousse. 'Tell me,' he said. 'Why are you here? What exactly *are* you doing in St. Castille?'

'I have already told you. I am here on holiday.'

Inspector Banyuls shrugged. 'I ask,' he said, 'because when you were brought in, this,' he reached into an inner pocket and withdrew another note-book which he tossed on to the end of the bed, 'this was found strapped to your ... er ... leg.' Once again Monsieur Pamplemousse was aware of an odd hesitation. 'It appears to contain entries about various rendez-vous—St. Castille included. All written in some kind of code. It is also,' he continued pointedly, 'full of holes.'

Monsieur Pamplemousse breathed a sigh of relief. To have had his true identity revealed would have been bad enough, but to have lost his precious note-book into the bargain would have been much, much worse. Its accumulation of riches would be hard to replace even though much of it had found its way into *Le Guide*.

He thought quickly. 'I am conducting a survey of the police forces of France,' he said maliciously. 'The holes are where I feel improvements could be made. If you look closely you will see there is a large one opposite St. Castille.'

But he was addressing a changed Inspector Banyuls. For some reason best known to himself he refused to be drawn. In any case, before he had time to reply the door opened and there was a rustle of starched linen as the ward sister—a nun—entered the room, signalling that it was time to leave. The door closed again and he heard a murmur of voices in the corridor outside. The sister appeared to be laying down the law regarding something about which Inspector Banyuls, to judge from the sceptical tone of his voice, remained unconvinced.

Monsieur Pamplemousse took stock of his surroundings. Obviously he was in some kind of hospice. Probably the one he'd seen on the edge of the town. From the view through the window he judged himself to be on an upper floor. A half-open door led to an adjoining bathroom. His suitcase was on a stand just inside the door. Slipping out of bed he crossed to it and lifted the lid. Everything appeared to be intact. Clothes, neatly folded, some untouched reading matter. A smaller case bearing an embossed stock pot on its lid, containing among other things his Leica R4 and Trinovid binoculars, property of *Le Guide,* was safe. The directeur would not have been pleased if on top of all else that had been lost. He unlocked the case, slipped the binoculars out of their compartment, and crossed to the window. His guess was correct. He was on the fifth floor. The window faced the mountains, affording much the same view as the one he'd enjoyed at La Langoustine. Somewhere out there in all probability was Doucette. Doucette and Pommes Frites.

He put the binoculars away again, relocked the case and climbed back into bed, slipping his feet beneath the wire cage which was the cause of the large lump at the bottom. He couldn't imagine why it was there. He felt his legs. Apart from a slight soreness where he'd been hit by the shot and the aggravation caused by Sophie's sandpapering, they seemed fine. In fact, taken all round, give or take a little stiffness here and there, he felt remarkably fit; none the worse for his fall.

He took a closer look at the room. On the wall near the door was a sampler. 'GOD GIVE ME PATIENCE', and underneath the words, 'BUT PLEASE MAKE IT SOON'. He was definitely in the hospice. The humour bore all the signs of a Catholic mind at work.

By his bed, on top of the cupboard, there was a glass and a bottle of Vichy water.

He sniffed. There was an all-pervading smell of flowers in the room, and yet he could see none.

Climbing out of bed for the second time, he pulled aside a screen across a corner near the window and identified the source.

Back in bed he stared at it, trying to decide what it could possibly mean. To say that he had been sent flowers was the understatement of the year. It looked like the entire stock of a *fleuriste*. There were flowers in vases and in jugs; there were posies, arrangements—someone had obviously gone to a great deal of trouble. In the middle of them all—the centrepiece in fact—was a large, glass-fronted cabinet containing, of all things, his wooden legs. He recognised the charred ends where the bed had caught fire. But why on earth had they been put inside a glass case? And why all the flowers? Above it there was a carved figurine of the crucifixion. It was like a shrine.

Monsieur Pamplemousse lay back pondering the matter for a while and he had almost fallen asleep again when he was woken by a tap on the door.

'Come in.' He sat up, rubbing his eyes drowsily and opened them to see a young novice coming towards him carrying a large parcel and some smaller mail: a packet and two postcards. She hovered uneasily beside the bed and then placed the parcel gingerly on the counterpane as if it was some kind of a bomb about to explode. Stepping back quickly, she blushed and then crossed herself. Her expression seemed to be a mixture of disbelief and disappointment. Rather as if yet another illusion in her young life had been shattered; her choice of calling confirmed.

He saw why. The parcel was from *Poupées Fantastiques*. The label would have been recognisable a kilometre away.

'Merci.' There seemed nothing else to say.

Monsieur Pamplemousse followed the girl with his eyes as she turned towards the glass cabinet, crossed herself a second time, and then fled from the room as if the Devil himself was behind her. Thank the Lord he was fit and well and not in there for treatment. If all the staff crossed themselves every time they did anything, woe betide anyone who was in there hoping for a quick operation.

He read the first of the two postcards. If the writing was familiar the words were equally so. It bore a Paris postmark and it was from Doucette in reply to the one he'd sent her when he arrived at La Langoustine. His own card, as always, had taken a good deal of time to write. He remembered it very clearly. 'This is a picture of my room (the one marked with a cross) and below it is the garden. Now they have a gazebo where every lunch time I sit and have my café and think of you.' Doucette's was brief and to the point. 'It is the same room you always stay in! Do they have no other cards?'

Monsieur Pamplemousse turned to the second one. On the front there was a picture of the Roman theatre at Orange and on the back another message from Doucette, this time full of regrets and wanting to see him. It must have been written while she was waiting for the *autobus* to St. Castille. Poor Doucette.

The packet was marked 'CONFIDENTIEL' and looked official. He tore the envelope open. The contents would have confirmed Banyuls' worst suspicions about his presence there. From a friend in ballistics, it dealt with the bullet case Pommes Frites had brought him the morning of the shooting in Place Napoleon.

It told him nothing that meant anything. It was much as he had expected. The cartridge was a 7.5 x 54 m.m. match quality. Probably fired from a French FR-F1 Tireur d'Elite sniper's rifle. Ten-shot, manually operated, bolt action. Now obsolete. There was a lot of other information about availability of silencers and other accessories, mostly technical and mostly meaningless. It was of a type common in the French Army, and doubtless on the black market as well; an observation confirmed by a newspaper cutting which was attached, reporting a recent raid on an Army barracks in the South where amongst others fifty such weapons had been stolen.

Monsieur Pamplemousse turned his attention to another newspaper cutting. This time from an Italian newspaper. There was a picture of a familiar figure waving two bandaged hands jubilantly in the air. Italian wasn't his strong suit, but as far as he could make out the cause of the celebration was the winning by Giampiero of his claim for damages against his employers. No figure was mentioned, simply the fact that a settlement had been reached out of court for a sum believed to be in excess of five thousand million Italian lire . . . that was . . . he did some quick mental arithmetic . . . that was more than twenty million French francs. No wonder Giampiero had said there was a lot at stake.

He stared at the cutting for a moment or two. Strange, but it was not quite as he had explained it. Giampiero hadn't mentioned it being settled out of court. He checked the date at the top. It was almost a year ago to the day. He looked at the item again. Unusually for an Italian paper, there was no human interest angle—just the bare facts. Perhaps by then the whole thing was already *passé*.

He lay back again and closed his eyes. In his mind he had already accepted the possibility that Giampiero was right and that he had become the target for, to use the well worn phrase, 'persons unknown'. There was no other explanation. Despite the fact that over the years he had on more than one occasion been the subject of an attack of revenge it had always been little more than a storm in a tea-cup. A temporary mental derangement of someone with a grudge to bear. If you carried on as usual it went away again, but this was different. The present series of attacks bore all the hallmarks of the Mafia; there was obviously more than one person involved—several in fact. The head he had been served up with on the first night had obviously been meant as a warning. Quite probably the attack on the hill the next day was meant that way too. If they had intended to kill him they would have used something more powerful than a shotgun.

The episode with the car? That was another matter again. It had been a narrow squeak, but he doubted very much if they had been out to kill him.

The sawing through of his balcony rails? Somehow that didn't fit in with the rest. It was an inconclusive thing to do, more the act of someone who wanted to get him out of the way for some reason or other.

He had his own theory as to the identity of the person responsible. The perfume that night in the toilet had been unmistakable, unique. The wearer, he knew, had the cold hard eyes of someone quite capable of wielding a hacksaw to good effect if the occasion demanded. Proving it would be another matter. Something Banyuls could have got his teeth into if he'd felt inclined, which he obviously didn't; his mind was on other things.

As for the bullet—the spent case for which even now lay on his bed—that, too, could have been an intended warning. Pommes Frites must have thought it important since he'd brought it back for him, and he trusted Pommes Frites' judgment in these matters.

His thoughts turned to Pommes Frites. He would never forgive himself if anything happened to him. Not that he thought for one moment that anything would. Pommes Frites was well able to take care of himself. Doucette he was even less worried about. Since he was so clearly the target, he and no one else, he couldn't believe that they would do her any harm. More than likely she would give as good as she got and they would be glad to be rid of her. Doucette had a sharp tongue when she was roused. All the same, he wouldn't get any peace until he saw both of them again alive and well.

Another strange thing was the lack of any note.

If what Giampiero had guessed at was true there should by now have been some kind of demand. At the very least after the first evening.

He wondered for a moment about Giampiero's relationship with Eva. On the surface it seemed an unlikely combination, and yet both in their own way were shadowy figures. Apart from a few brief encounters in the restaurant he'd hardly set eyes on the girl since he arrived; at least he had talked to Giampiero. Of the two he instinctively liked and trusted Giampiero, and yet . . .

Monsieur Pamplemousse picked up his pen. It was time for a list. A setting out of all the relevant facts in chronological order, beginning with his arrival on the Monday evening.

What day did Banyuls say it was now? Friday? It was incredible to think that he'd been in St. Castille for less than four whole days. So much had happened it felt more like a month.

But before he had time to marshal his thoughts, let alone put pen to paper, he heard the sound of approaching voices in the corridor. Lots of voices. They paused outside his room. It sounded like some kind of delegation. *Mon Dieu!* What was it now?

He hadn't long to wait. The door burst open and a flood of white-coated students poured through. Led by the large and authoritative figure of a surgeon and accompanied by the sister and a younger nun carrying some X-ray plates, they headed towards his bed.

Totally ignoring him, they gathered round the foot and waited expectantly while the sister untucked the top sheet.

'*Voilà!*' Taking the end from her, the surgeon

threw it back over the top of the cage like a conjuror demonstrating his latest and most ambitious trick.

If a flock of pigeons had emerged Monsieur Pamplemousse couldn't have been more taken aback, and he was hardly prepared for the response accorded this relatively simple act.

The applause as the audience bent down to take a closer look was spontaneous and genuine. Mingled with it there was a feeling of awe, almost as if those present felt they were witnessing some big breakthrough in the medical world; a moment of truth to which they had been admitted as privileged beings.

Given the cool draught which had suddenly blown up beneath his nightshirt, Monsieur Pamplemousse felt he hardly warranted such appreciation, gratifying though it was.

But his moment of glory was short-lived. Leaving the bedclothes to fall where they might, the surgeon strode across to the window and signalled for the X-ray plates.

Levering himself up in bed, Monsieur Pamplemousse strained in vain to get a better view. Nor, for that matter, could he catch more than a few passing words, and those that did come his way were hardly reassuring.

Lowering his voice in the manner of doctors the world over when discussing the fate of their patients, the surgeon held forth while the others gathered round him like members of a rugby scrum. If Monsieur Pamplemousse had thrown a ball in—or better still, the bed pan—he felt sure it would have come flying out again.

There were a lot of sucking-in noises as one or

two of the students drew breath in surprise and several times he caught the word *amputer*. It was a word that seemed to bother the sister almost as much as it did him, but for very different reasons. It wasn't so much that she was against the idea; she didn't want it to happen before the arrival of the *évêque*. Though what he would want with a bishop, or a bishop with him, Monsieur Pamplemousse had no idea.

A second school of thought seemed to favour a series of exploratory operations in the interim period. *Découvert* was the word used.

Monsieur Pamplemousse had a profound mistrust of the medical profession. They had a habit of removing things without so much as a by-your-leave, or even a second's thought as to whether or not they could get them all back in again, and he had no wish to be tampered with unless there was a very good reason.

Finally, he was unable to stand it a moment longer.

'When, or how, or why I arrived in this hospital,' he bellowed, 'I have no idea. But I arrived with at least one of everything to which I am entitled, two where there should be two, and that is how I intend leaving. I demand to see whoever is in charge immediately. I know my rights.'

Silence greeted his outburst for a second or two. Even the surgeon was momentarily struck dumb. Obviously, the thought of a patient having any kind of rights was an entirely new concept, and one outside his experience.

The sister hurried forward, anxious to pour oil on troubled waters. 'Now, now, we mustn't behave like that.'

'*We?*' barked Monsieur Pamplemousse. '*We* are not. *I* am. And I repeat, I am having no more tablets, no more injections, no more talk of exploratory operations, no more anything until I learn exactly what is going on.

'As for you, Monsieur.' He glared across at the surgeon. 'If you or any of your colleagues come within a kilometre of me with one of your wretched knives, or if I hear the word *amputer* once more it will be you who are in need of a transplant, not me. I hesitate to go into details while there are ladies present, but by the time I have finished you may well wish to join them in taking the vow.'

Not displeased with his effort, Monsieur Pamplemousse lay back in his bed again with his hands clasped and watched while his visitors filed out looking suitably cowed.

As soon as they had disappeared he reached over and poured himself some Vichy water. Being in hospital was improving neither his temper nor his liver.

He was about to return to his list when there was yet another knock at the door. He closed his eyes. Let them all come. It was getting to be like the Gare de Lyon at the start of the holiday season. Who was it to be this time?

The answer was framed in the doorway. It was Inspector Banyuls again. The new, conciliatory Banyuls. A Banyuls, nevertheless, who, catching sight of the parcel on the bed, couldn't resist a dig.

'*Sacrebleu!*' he exclaimed. 'You never give up, Pamplemousse. Even in hospital, you never give up.'

Monsieur Pamplemousse tried mentally counting up to ten. He wondered whether the inspector had taken some sort of course for saying the wrong thing or whether it just came naturally. If he had taken a course he must undoubtedly have come out top of his year.

The inevitable note-book appeared. 'You will be pleased to know, Pamplemousse, that progress has been made.'

Monsieur Pamplemousse felt his heart miss a beat. His opinion of Banyuls went up. 'You mean . . . Doucette? Pommes Frites has found Doucette?'

Inspector Banyuls shook his head. He seemed to find the interruption annoying. 'We have found your car battery!'

'My battery?' Monsieur Pamplemousse repeated the words as if in a dream.

'I thought you would be pleased. It appears to have been damaged in some way. I doubt if it is usable. We found it in a local garage. Whoever was responsible for the theft brought it in on the back of a bicycle and changed it for a new one suitable for a Deux Chevaux.

'What is more, we have a very full description of the person. Make no mistake. We shall bring him to book.'

Monsieur Pamplemousse lay very still, trying to make up his mind whether the inspector was being serious or not. He decided that incredible though it was he had yet to match the description in his note-book with the patient in front of him. But Inspector Banyuls obviously had other things on his mind.

Putting his note-book away, he approached the end of the bed.

'May I?' he enquired. And without waiting for a

reply he lifted up the counterpane and peered underneath.

'Curious,' he said. 'Most curious. You will not mind if we send someone round to photograph them?'

'Them?' A dreadful thought entered Monsieur Pamplemousse's mind. Perhaps he had suffered some terrible injury. An injury so bad no one had dared tell him. He dismissed the idea, but only with difficulty.

'Let them all come,' he said, putting on a brave face. 'I am past caring. All I wish for at the moment is that someone should tell me what is going on. Not a single person comes into this room without they lift up my bed-sheets. I am beginning to feel like some side-show in a travelling circus.'

It was Inspector Banyuls' turn to look puzzled. 'You mean . . . you really do not know?'

'That is exactly what I mean.'

Inspector Banyuls crossed to the window and stood for a moment looking out in silence, then he turned. When he spoke again he was obviously choosing his words with care.

'The people in this part of the world are people of the mountains. They are insular—like islanders. Suspicious of strangers, and very superstitious.'

Monsieur Pamplemousse listened with interest. He couldn't for the life of him think what the other was leading up to.

'Some say one thing, some another. Rumours are rife. There are those, like the good Mother Superior, who maintain that it is the work of God. Others say the opposite. Already a maid in the hotel has come forward to give evidence of things she has seen. She has produced part of a mattress

149

with a hole burned in the middle to substantiate her views. A statement has been taken. Speaking for myself, I am keeping an open mind.'

Monsieur Pamplemousse ground his teeth. 'Banyuls,' he said, slowly and deliberately, 'you are a good man, but will you please stop beating about the bush and answer my question. Why am I being kept in here?'

The inspector moved away from the window and placed himself in a strategic position between the bed and the door. He pointed towards the glass case in the corner. 'You are here,' he said, 'for the very simple reason that yesterday afternoon when you fell from your balcony you were a man with two wooden legs. Moments later, when you were found, you had two real ones. It is not every day the people of St. Castille are privileged to bear witness to a miracle in their midst.

'There is, of course, a third faction—the disbelievers, or should I say the *agnostiques*.' He shrugged. 'But then, there always will be, whatever the subject.'

Monsieur Pamplemousse couldn't resist the obvious question.

'And you, Banyuls, to which faction do you belong?'

'I am a policeman. I deal in facts. I am also by nature suspicious and I keep an open mind. What do you say, Pamplemousse?'

Monsieur Pamplemousse clasped his hands in front of him and assumed one of his most beatific smiles. Now that he had recovered from the initial shock of the inspector's revelation a certain something inside him felt he might enjoy the almost unlimited possibilities of his new role.

'Peace be with you, my son,' he intoned. 'For blessed are they who have not seen and yet still choose to believe.'

As the bang from the door echoed and re-echoed down the corridor he relaxed again. The smile faded as he returned to his list. Baiting Banyuls was all very well but it didn't solve any of his problems; rather the reverse.

Tearing off the top sheet of his note-pad he wrote the words 'I MUST BE KIND TO BANYULS' in large letters and attached it to the light on the wall behind his head. In that position it would announce to all the world that deep down his heart was in the right place and yet it would retain the advantage of not being permanently in his line of vision.

9

Friday Afternoon

Unbeknown to Monsieur Pamplemousse, his feelings about Inspector Banyuls were being echoed at that very moment by Pommes Frites. If someone had posed the direct question, 'Hands up all those who wish they had been kinder to Inspector Banyuls,' Pommes Frites would have lost no time in raising his right paw. Pommes Frites was in a situation where he could have used some assistance. Something in the nature of a fan-out by the local gendarmerie would have gone down very well at that moment in time, for although his early training with the Sûreté had taught him many things, the art of being in more than one place at the same time had not been included in his course syllabus.

Had Pommes Frites been in the habit of keeping a diary, he would undoubtedly have headed the day in large, capital letters: 'BLACK FRIDAY'. One way and another it had been a fitting follow-on from

'DARK GREY THURSDAY', 'BROWN WEDNES-
DAY', 'OCHRE TUESDAY' and 'PUCE MONDAY'.

Not that he was grumbling. On and off, he'd had
quite an enjoyable week. The taste of some of the
meals at La Langoustine still lingered, and there
had been some pleasant strolls round the town
itself. But the ratio of good moments to bad had
followed a downward curve as the week progressed,
culminating in his present dilemma. To paraphrase
Shakespeare's *Hamlet*, it really boiled down to a
question of, 'To go or not to go? Whether 'twas
better to keep a watchful eye on Madame Pamplemousse and suffer the possible slings and bullets
of her outraged captors, or, having spent most of a
day and a night on the job, hot foot it back to town
by the shortest possible route.'

His pursuit of the lorry had got off to a bad start.
At first he'd been so taken aback at seeing Madame Pamplemousse take off in the gazebo he'd
hardly been able to believe his eyes. Then, when
the full import of what was going on finally sank
in, he'd stood up too quickly in his excitement and
got himself entangled with his kennel.

His state of shock had been compounded when
his master had, quite literally, landed at his feet.
For the second time in as many days he'd found
himself staring at the remains of his house. The
only consolation to be gained was that in struggling to free himself from his kennel he'd quite by
chance pushed it into exactly the right spot to
break Monsieur Pamplemousse's fall and save him,
if not from death, at least from serious injury.

By the time he'd checked things out and assured
himself with a few well chosen licks that his mas-

ter was still breathing, he had lost even more time and the lorry was nowhere in sight.

Pommes Frites was good at trails, but in the absence of any kind of scent he'd had to rely on instinct, and in the end instinct hadn't let him down.

He knew that the lorry had gone in roughly the same direction as the one he and his master had taken the morning of the attack, so he took a chance. There was certainly a smell of lorries. Not that there was anything unusual in that. There was scarcely a ditch or hedgerow in the whole of France that didn't bear silent witness to the fact that lorries in one form or another passed by every day of the year, but the smell he chose to follow was unhealthily fresh.

The first part of the journey took him up the same road, past the very same bush which had caused all the trouble. Pommes Frites had given the bush a wide berth, even though it was now lying on its side, its foliage turning brown. He had no wish to repeat the experience.

All the same, it gave him his bearings, and he was able to take a short cut over the brow of the hill until a point in the road where it suddenly branched into two.

It was here that luck deserted him temporarily. Taking the right fork—the one that appeared the most used—he went on up the mountain towards the site of the new solar heating station. There he'd spent a fruitless day sniffing around domes and bits of metal and vast areas of glass and getting hotter and hotter in the process.

Hotter and hotter, that is, until the sun had gone

down. After which he'd got colder and colder. The temperature dropped considerably and Pommes Frites spent a sleepless night wondering what to do next.

But all had not been in vain. In fact, if he hadn't gone off on a false trail and reached his vantage point he might never have seen the flash of morning sun reflected from a piece of glass on a neighbouring hill. It had to be the gazebo.

Pommes Frites made his way back down to the fork and then set off again, happy in the knowledge that what goes up must eventually come down again, and that since the road, which had now become a track, didn't seem to go anywhere other than up, anything like a lorry would have to pass him if it came back down again. It was a tenuous piece of reasoning, but when you are running hard reasoning comes in short spurts, and Pommes Frites had been running very hard indeed.

It all took much longer than he had expected and it wasn't until he was almost at the highest point of the next hill that he rounded a bend and suddenly stopped dead in his tracks. There in front of him, large as life and parked outside a small stone building, was the lorry. Crouching down behind a boulder, he surveyed the scene, taking it all in bit by bit and building up a picture in his mind. Somehow or other it wasn't quite as he had expected.

True, the gazebo had been unloaded from the lorry. It had been manhandled down some planks which still rested on the tailboard, and it was now ensconced on a nearby hillock.

But it wasn't the lorry or the gazebo that caused Pommes Frites to give the bloodhound's equivalent of a double-take; it was the sight of its lone occupant.

He could hardly believe his eyes. He'd been prepared for practically anything but what he saw. He tried looking away again and then refocusing his gaze, but it was still exactly the same.

Far from being in a distressed condition, Madame Pamplemousse appeared to be enjoying herself no end. The door of the gazebo was wide open and she was sitting in the middle, basking in the rays of the morning sun as it beat down on her through the glass roof and sides. She even had her coat off which was most unusual. Pommes Frites couldn't remember ever having seen Madame Pamplemousse out of doors without a coat before. He was too far away to see exactly what she was doing, but if it hadn't been quite so hard to believe he would have sworn she was knitting. By her side there was a breakfast tray.

While he was watching a man came out of the hut carrying another tray which he took across to the gazebo. He was followed by a second man who hurried on ahead to prepare the way. There was a flurry of movement and then a short scene which Pommes Frites immediately recognised. It was one he'd seen enacted many times before. He knew it off by heart. The straightening of the back, the wagging finger. He could almost hear the sniff which punctuated the monologue. The men were being told off for entering the gazebo without first wiping the dust from their shoes. Even as he watched one of them bent down and began wiping the floor with his handkerchief.

Madame Pamplemousse might have been abducted, but she was quite definitely in charge, and it was equally clear that she was perfectly happy to stay where she was—at least for the time being.

Taking advantage of the moment, Pommes Frites crept nearer still, wriggling along on all fours, body close to the ground, until he was in a position to get a better view and hear what was going on.

It was hard to know exactly what was being said—a lot of the conversation seemed to be conducted in sign language, but the gist was clear enough: Madame Pamplemousse was being invited to return to St. Castille the way she had come. Equally clearly Madame Pamplemousse had no intention whatsoever of doing anything of the sort. Madame Pamplemousse had had quite enough of travelling on the back of lorries. She was never going to travel on the back of a lorry again. Either they provided her with proper transport or she would not go at all. And if she didn't go at all then it would be the worse for all concerned.

There was a hurried conference. Lesser beings might well have been left to their fate, but Madame Pamplemousse was not, in any sense of the word, a lesser being. Madame Pamplemousse was not to be trifled with. What Madame Pamplemousse said went.

Under other circumstances Pommes Frites might well have enjoyed the sight of his adversaries being so thoroughly cowed, but he had various things on his mind.

Apart from being a bit fed up at having spent a night without food and shelter on the mountain, he was beginning to wonder how his master was getting on. For the time being, Madame Pamplemousse seemed in no great danger, and at least he now knew where she was, which was more than he could say for his master. There was no knowing where he might be.

Something else was beginning to bother him as well, another mathematical problem. Of the two men, he recognised one as the man who had sprung out of the bush at him—the one who had gone off bang so unexpectedly. The second man had been driving the car the night when he had very nearly been run down, of that he was sure. Pommes Frites had a good memory for faces. But one and one made two, and there had been three people in the car. The one who was missing was the man who had appeared briefly as the waiter on their first night. Of the three Pommes Frites trusted him least of all. He had a nasty feeling his absence might have something to do with his master, but first he had to find Monsieur Pamplemousse, and to find Monsieur Pamplemousse he had to get back to St. Castille, and quickly. Pommes Frites' thought processes might have been slow but they were thorough; they left no stone unturned, and once he'd sorted things out in his mind he was quick to take action. A moment later he was on his way back down the mountain as fast as his legs would carry him.

As it happened, Monsieur Pamplemousse's thoughts at that moment were occupied by much more mundane matters.

Hardly had Inspector Banyuls left than a trolley arrived bearing his lunch. After an evening and a night without food, Monsieur Pamplemousse was more than ready for it; now he was regretting his haste.

Not even several copious draughts of Vichy water helped to assuage the pain which had settled heavily in the middle of his chest, a pain which was only relieved by getting out of bed and walking around.

He crossed to the window and gazed out gloomily. One day he would have to persuade the directeur to allow him to conduct a survey of food in institutions. One day. It would hardly be a labour of love. The string which had held his *poulet* together had been better cooked than the bird itself. As for the soup that preceded it . . . what was it the Prince of Gastronomes, Curmonsky, had said? A good soup should taste of the things it is made of. If the one he had just eaten fulfilled that criterion he shuddered to think what its ingredients must have been.

In the courtyard below him people were hurrying to and fro. An ambulance drew up and disgorged its occupants. There was a sprinkling of nuns. Monsieur Pamplemousse's gaze softened as he looked at them. They were good people, devoting their lives to others. They always made him feel a trifle inadequate. A car drew up a short distance away from the others and a woman in black got out. The sight of all the comings and goings made him feel restless. The whole thing was quite ridiculous, but having said that the question arose as to what he should or even could do about it.

To walk out of the hospital was one thing. To leave quietly without setting up a great hue and cry was another matter entirely.

He crossed to the door and opened it. A long corridor running the full length of the building stretched out before him. The stairs and lifts were at the far end, on either side of a glass-fronted room inside which he could see the sister busy at her desk. As she looked up, sensing a movement, he dodged back into his room.

Glancing at the crumpled bed with its cage for his legs and the pile of pillows, a thought struck him; memories of childhood pranks and days at summer camps. A momentary diversion was all that was needed and he could be away.

He was on the point of stripping off the bedclothes when another idea occurred to him. A refinement which might make all the difference between success and failure. Once again *Poupées Fantastiques* could come to his rescue.

Bereft of Pommes Frites' gas cylinder, Monsieur Pamplemousse had to resort to what amounted to mouth-to-mouth resuscitation and by the time he had finished he was red in the face and panting from his exertions.

All the same, it had definitely been worthwhile. *Poupées Fantastiques* had excelled themselves. True, they had omitted the wooden legs this time, but in the circumstances that suited his purpose very well. If things carried on at the present rate they must be considering going into mass production. He would have to demand a royalty for the use of his image. He was pleased to see that they had taken note of his complaint and this time they had included the batteries. Twelve, no less! And he could see why. The Mark V differed from its predecessors in details only, but those details had obviously inspired the designers to give full rein to their fantasies. A fact which was readily apparent when he operated the switch.

He drew the blinds and then, to complete the

picture, slipped out of his nightshirt. It was as he was in the act of pulling it over the head of the dummy that he heard voices outside.

Flinging the model on to the bed, he made a dive for the safety of the screen in the corner of the room. No sooner was he behind it than the door opened and he heard the voice of the girl who'd brought the mail earlier in the day.

'There is a lady to see you, Monsieur Pample-mousse . . .'

The voice broke off in mid-sentence and he heard a gasp. Peering through a join in the screen he saw the white face of the novice gazing in horror at the figure on the bed. In his haste he must have left the motor switched on.

'Oh, *Mon Dieu*!' Crossing herself, the girl fled from the room, leaving Monsieur Pamplemousse's visitor to her fate.

A moment later there was a click as the door was gently closed. His visitor clearly didn't share the novice's inhibitions. A thought crossed Monsieur Pamplemousse's mind. Could it be . . . ? He shifted his position to try and get a better view and received an impression of blackness, a black veil, a black hat, and a long black dress reaching right to the ground.

Whoever it was, it certainly wasn't Sophie; and yet, even as he watched there was a flurry of movement and before his astonished gaze the un-identified visitor picked up the hem of her dress with both hands and began to raise it. Monsieur Pamplemousse crouched rooted to the spot. If it wasn't Madame Sophie it must be a near relation. An aunt perhaps? It was incredible, the woman hadn't been in the room more than a minute. He wondered if it had something to do with the mountain air.

But if Monsieur Pamplemousse was expecting to witness an action replay of the occurrences in his own room he was doomed to disappointment. Instead of revealing a set of frilly underwear, the first thing that caught his eye was a matching pair of blue trouser legs, rolled up to calf length and held in place by a pair of clothes pegs. The second thing, dangling from a fastening concealed beneath the dress, was the ominous shape of a Walther 9mm submachine-gun. It was a type Monsieur Pamplemousse had once fired during an attachment to the West German police; he remembered it well.

Slowly and deliberately the owner swung the stock into position, cocked the gun, slipped the lever above the pistol grip to fully automatic and pointed it towards the bed.

With a rate of fire of 550 rounds a minute, the full magazine took a mere seventeen seconds to discharge, nevertheless it seemed to last an eternity. It gave Monsieur Pamplemousse time to thank his lucky stars that he was where he was and not still between the sheets. Had he been in the bed . . . his stomach turned to water at the thought.

Luckily the gun was equipped with a silencer or the noise would have been deafening. Even so it was loud enough for Monsieur Pamplemousse to expect to hear running feet at any moment, but none came. Perhaps, for once, the sister had deserted her post.

The assailant was in no great hurry. If anything he seemed to be acting as if he had all the time in the world. For a full thirty seconds he gazed through the smoke at the remains of the figure on the bed. Although Monsieur Pamplemousse had no means of knowing it, his would-be assailant had just received the answer to a question that had often been a subject for discussion among those who worried about such things. If a man died at what might be called a *moment critique*, did he or did he not retain his enthusiasm for matters of the flesh. The answer in this particular case was definitely no. He had never seen anyone's manhood quite so destroyed. It was all very satisfactory. It was a pity the matter had to end this way, but that was life—or, in this case, death. You won one—you lost another. His instructions in the beginning had been to warn, to intimidate, but not to kill. However, there came a time when matters got out of hand, when tidiness was important. This was one of those occasions. He would have to wait a little while longer for his rewards, but he had all the time in the world. Waiting—in the company of 'a certain person', would have its compensations.

He smiled grimly beneath the veil, then as slowly and as deliberately as when he'd entered the room, he detached the umbilical-like cord from the gun and placed it on the floor. Walking would be much easier without it—he had no wish to have a hot barrel between his legs. A moment later he crept out of the room as silently as he had arrived.

Monsieur Pamplemousse let a decent interval elapse before he came out from behind the screen. The air was heavy with the smell of cordite. Avoiding the cartridge cases that had been ejected on to the floor, he crossed to the window, threw up the blind and leaned out.

Taking a deep breath of the fresh air he turned

back into the room. As he did so he saw the door handle turning. Suddenly conscious of his vulnerable state now that his nightshirt had been destroyed by gunfire, he made a dive for the safety of the screen. He was only just in time.

'At it again, Pamplemousse?' Inspector Banyuls made no attempt to conceal his disapproval. 'Is there no limit to your depravity? I have received a serious complaint from the Mother Superior. It seems that you have been exposing yourself to one of the novices. These young ladies have taken the vow . . .'

The voice broke off in mid-flight. Very gently Monsieur Pamplemousse lowered himself to the floor in order to get a better view. But he needn't have worried about making too much noise. The inspector's attention was totally riveted by something just out of the line of vision.

For a moment or two Monsieur Pamplemousse wondered what could possibly be of such paramount importance it took precedence even over the contents of the bed. Clearly, it was having a deeply emotional effect on the other.

Then he remembered. It was his 'thought for the day'; the one he had fixed to the wall before lunch. 'I MUST BE KIND TO BANYULS.'

He hesitated, wondering whether to make his presence known, but before he had time to make up his mind there came the sound of a car starting up. It was followed almost immediately by an instantly recognisable barking.

The spell was broken. Inspector Banyuls pulled himself together, rushed to the window and looked out. Then, moving at a pace which Monsieur Pamplemousse would not previously have given him credit for, he disappeared out of the room like a man possessed.

As the pounding of feet died away Monsieur Pamplemousse hopped over to the window and peered over the edge. He was in time to see the car which had arrived earlier bearing his would-be assassin disappear out of the gate at high speed. A moment later Inspector Banyuls emerged from the main entrance, hurled himself into his own car and followed after it.

'Pommes Frites! Pommes Frites! *Asseyez-vous! Asseyez-vous!*'

Monsieur Pamplemousse's voice coming from on high caused Pommes Frites to skid to a halt. Pommes Frites liked chases and he'd been about to set off on yet another one. Hopefully it would have ended with him being able to slot a further piece of his jig-saw puzzle of a problem into place, for it took more than a frock and a veil and a hat to disguise the fact that he'd been in the presence of the last member of the gang.

But hearing his master's voice and knowing that he was safe and well was much more important. That took precedence over all else.

He was pleased that on the off chance he'd followed Inspector Banyuls. Having drawn a blank at La Langoustine as well as several other likely places in the town, he'd begun to get worried. It had been something of a forlorn hope, but the inspector did have a habit of turning up unexpectedly and he'd had a feeling that where he was his master wouldn't be far away.

Now all he had to do was find out where the voice was coming from.

He hadn't long to wait. There was a clattering of

feet and Monsieur Pamplemousse came out of the hospice to greet him.

For a moment or two all was panting and licking tongues. Then Pommes Frites bounded towards the gate, narrowly missing being run over by an ambulance that was coming the other way.

As he rushed off up the road barking his head off, Monsieur Pamplemousse hesitated. Short of phoning for a taxi and saying 'Follow two cars which went that way about ten minutes ago,' he wasn't at all sure what to do next.

Pommes Frites was sure. As he came bounding back to his master and nuzzled up to him, licking him in no uncertain way, he made his feelings very clear. Pommes Frites was hungry.

Monsieur Pamplemousse looked at his watch. Lunch came early in the hospice; his own had been shortly after mid-day. It was now approaching two o'clock. In the circumstances it might be best to leave the next moves to those whose job it was to worry about such things.

He wondered whether they should eat at La Langoustine or the Bar du Centre, then reached for his note-book. If his memory served him correctly, there was a little place up in the mountains—about twenty minutes drive away, where they often had *Lapin au Gratin* on the menu. Rabbit marinated in white wine, then cooked gently for an hour or so with thyme and garlic, before being coated thickly with white breadcrumbs and cheese and browned under a hot grill. If he was lucky they might have it today. He'd be interested in seeing Pommes Frites' reactions. His taste buds began to water. He was glad he'd left most of his chicken. Hunger was the best sauce in the world.

As for the other matter; no doubt all would be revealed in the fullness of time and he was perfectly content to wait.

10

SATURDAY

MONSIEUR PAMPLEMOUSSE WAS WHISTLING as he left the offices of the P.T.T. Returning his *poupées*—one charred beyond belief, the other full of holes—had been a symbolic act; like the tearing up of papers and the tidying of his desk in his days at the Quai des Orfévres when he'd reached the end of a case.

The idea had come to him when he found a packing slip in the second parcel. 'In case of complaint,' it said, 'return within fourteen days and your money will be refunded.' He wondered what *Poupées Fantastiques* would make of them, not to mention the two burst kennels. Not for one moment did he expect to get his money back, but the action made him feel better and at least it solved the problem of what to do with the remains.

The whistling was also a sure sign that it was nearly time to move on. Pommes Frites recognised the fact at once, even if his master didn't.

Outside in the square things were much as usual for a Saturday morning. A couple waiting for the *autobus* recognised them and nudged each other. Their interest communicated itself to others in the queue and there was a ripple of turning heads. An old woman in black came out of the mini *supermarché* pushing a chariot laden with packets of soap powder, crossed herself when she saw them and turned up an alleyway. He took a quick photograph before she disappeared from view. A small boy came running up to ask for an autograph. Monsieur Pamplemousse obliged, thinking himself lucky he wasn't a pop star having to do it all the time. With a name like Pamplemousse he'd soon get writer's cramp. The boy thanked him and then looked disappointed when he saw the paper, as though he'd been expecting something more. Perhaps he ought to have added Pommes Frites' paw print for good measure.

He glanced at his watch. Ten thirty. Time for a quick stroll before his meeting with Giampiero, time to put together a picnic.

As they made their way down the Grande Avenue Charles de Gaulle for the last time they received more curious glances. A café went quiet, then started up again as soon as they were past. Some people crossed the road to take a closer look, others made efforts to avoid them. Monsieur Pamplemousse found himself walking self-consciously, in much the same way as he always did if he was involved in any kind of theatricals. He couldn't have felt more awkward if he'd actually possessed wooden legs. Madame Peigné was looking hopefully out of her shop window. Pommes Frites obliged, drawing on some of his infinite reserves.

169

By the time they got back to the Square du Centre the *autobus* had been and gone. There was a large van outside Monsieur Dupré's. Four men, looking like mime artists as they struggled with their invisible load, were fitting a new window into place.

Monsieur Pamplemousse climbed up the steps to the hotel terrace, selected a table a little apart from the others, and ordered *café* for two. He had a feeling Giampiero would be on time. Pommes Frites had a quick drink from the fountain, repaid some of it in kind on the side, then joined him.

Inside the hotel, through one of the dining room windows, he could see the staff getting ready for a wedding party that afternoon, arranging flowers, setting tables together in a long row, lining up the glasses meticulously. He caught a glimpse of Madame Sophie supervising. Doubtless it was a scene which was being enacted all over France that morning. It was the time of year for weddings.

He thought of Doucette and wondered how she was getting on. Despite all the activity in the hotel, Auguste had still found time to take her back up to the gazebo after breakfast on the pretext that he wanted to check on his property. Monsieur Pamplemousse suspected he wanted to pump her on the subject of his Stock Pot rating. Knowing Doucette he wouldn't get very far. They rarely discussed such matters anyway.

Auguste had returned with the news that it would need a small crane and a lorry to get the gazebo back down again and reinstalled. In the meantime Madame Pamplemousse was happy. She was hoping to finish another sleeve before lunch.

At eleven o'clock precisely Giampiero appeared

on the steps of the hotel. Monsieur Pamplemousse noted regretfully that he was alone. He'd been hoping to meet the delectable Eva, but he had a feeling that was now something which wasn't to be.

Giampiero looked like a new man, as indeed he was in at least one respect. It gave them something in common.

He held out his hand in greeting as he came towards the table. Monsieur Pamplemousse grasped it warmly in his own, retaining his hold for perhaps a fraction longer than he normally would have done, making sure it was real. Not to be outdone, he crossed his legs as he sat down, revealing a few inches of calf. It didn't pass unnoticed.

Giampiero settled down beside him. 'And Madame Pamplemousse, how is she this morning? None the worse for her experience, I trust?'

'On the contrary. She hasn't enjoyed herself so much in years. It is quite like old times. She is spending the day at what she calls her "mountain retreat". I swear it is the first time I have seen her take her coat off out of doors in the twenty years we have been married. Not only that, but she will be able to do her meditating in peace. It is like having her own little temple on top of a mountain. She is determined to stay there until it is taken away.'

The words came out automatically. It was like the beginning of a fencing match; there were little preliminaries to be got through, niceties to be observed, whereas in truth there were so many things he wanted to know he was dying to get on with the main purpose of the meeting.

'And you? You are still planning to leave?'

'Pommes Frites and I have another appointment,' said Monsieur Pamplemousse non-committally. He tossed the question back. 'How about you?'

'I shall return to Rome. I, too, have another appointment. I may take a few days off to get used to these again.' Giampiero lifted up both hands and flexed his muscles. The fingers looked pinched and white where they had been compressed by the steel claws, as if he was suffering from advanced anaemia.

'It is surprisingly difficult. I keep reaching for things and stopping short. Shaving is the worst. I suppose you get used to anything in time, but it has given me a new outlook on life. I shall never again pass by a beggar without arms.'

'If it were me I think it would take more than a few days,' said Monsieur Pamplemousse.

Giampiero shrugged. He gazed out across the square. Already a group of men were getting ready for a game of *boules,* surveying the ground; kicking aside stones, polishing their equipment with pieces of old towelling.

'I shall also have to get used to being "single" again.'

They both fell silent, each busy with his own thoughts.

The revelation when they'd met earlier that morning that Giampiero worked as an investigator for one of the big Italian insurance companies had not come as too much of a surprise. It fitted the facts. Now that his work was over he'd slipped into his normal character, much as Monsieur Pamplemousse might have donned a favourite sports jacket.

What still staggered him, though, was the business of the steel claws; the fact that the hands had been artificial in all senses of the word. It took a bit of getting used to. Giampiero looked naked without them. Like a man who has just shaved off his beard.

He gazed curiously at the other. The world of insurance was an alien one to him. He'd once put in a minor claim after a burglary, but it had been turned down on the grounds that he'd left his window open—a window on the seventh floor! Since then he'd treated all insurance companies with suspicion; they were a law unto themselves, the very first to cry wolf if they suspected anyone was trying to do them down, inventors of the small print, masters of the escape clause. But this was clearly something different again. It must have been a no-expense-spared operation, far removed from anything he'd ever had to deal with in the Sûreté.

'It would be interesting to hear your story. I promise it will go no further.'

Giampiero poured himself another coffee. 'There was money at stake. Big money. It was not the first claim Eva had made on the group. Hopefully it will be the last. Insurance companies do not like being taken for a ride and they have very long memories.'

'How many were there, then?' ventured Monsieur Pamplemousse. 'Claims, I mean.'

'This would have been the fourth, if you count the first, legitimate one; each larger than the one before. This time it wasn't so much a claim as a "misappropriation of funds", but it would have amounted to the same thing in the end.' Giampiero sipped his coffee, then added some sugar.

'Eva G. 92-62-92. Height 172 centimetres. Weight 40.82 kilos. Caucasian blonde. Swedish. Born

Saltsjöbaden—a small town outside Stockholm, of respectable middle-class parents. Small scar above left ear from an early skiing accident. Birthmark behind right upper thigh.'

The facts were reeled off from memory in the way most men might have talked of their cars.

'At fifteen she went to stay with a rich uncle in Berlin who promised to complete her education. His idea of completing it was to jump into bed with her the first night she arrived. Ten minutes later her hatred of men was born. Two years later she got her revenge by marrying him. Two years after that he got his revenge. He died, but the money he had promised her in his will went instead to a Home for Destitute Women, with a rider saying that he hoped she would benefit in the fullness of time. Her hatred of men was now absolute.

'Suddenly, she found herself alone and without money, so she looked around and soon discovered that the world—especially the international playgrounds of Italy and the South of France—is well blessed with the rich and the elderly and the lonely, many of whom are only too pleased to receive the attentions of the young and the beautiful. It pleases their vanity and they can afford the price. There are many to choose from and, believe me, when Eva set her mind to it she could be very alluring. She could take her pick.'

'I believe you.' Monsieur Pamplemousse thought back to the very first evening. Despite the row he remembered finding it hard to keep his eyes off her. There had been many others in the room who would have been only too pleased to have been the object of her attentions. Supposing it had been her making a play for him and not Madame Sophie? What then?

'Her second husband she met in Cannes. He, poor devil, fell off his yacht shortly after marrying her, but not before he'd taken out a heavy insurance in her favour.

'The inquest returned an open verdict. A little too much to drink. A dark night. A slippery gang-plank. No one saw it happen. The company paid up, but at the same time they put a little red star on her file.

'When, a few years later, her third husband met an untimely end—this time in a road accident—a head-on collision with a lorry on a mountain road in Tuscany, the file was left out.

'Eva had made her second big mistake in choosing another company within the same group so soon after her first claim. Her first mistake was in getting more greedy, but having tasted the good life she found it impossible to give up.

'Again, through lack of evidence, the insurance company had to pay up in the end, but it was noted that soon after she collected the money large sums were withdrawn from her account and certain payments were made to persons unknown. The money was "laundered" as they say, and by a very roundabout route ended up not far from where it started. Other people began to get interested. The tax authorities. Interpol.

'So, plans were laid, and that was where I came on the scene. The first accident was set up, then the second. The right amount of publicity was generated and after a suitable interval an introduction arranged.'

'How did you know she would fall for it? You couldn't have been sure.'

Giampiero smiled. 'Greed is a great motivator. By then Eva was getting a bit fed up with the kind of life she was leading. It isn't all that much fun playing nursemaid to geriatric millionaires. She jumped at the chance of a younger man. In a way, I quite enjoyed playing the part of the helpless *ingénu* who has suddenly acquired undreamed of wealth and doesn't know how to handle it. As a student of human nature you must agree that given the sum involved the probability of its succeeding was pretty high.

'Soon after we were married I began to make it grow sour. I developed a mean streak which Eva didn't like at all.'

Monsieur Pamplemousse tried to picture the scene. 'Weren't you afraid you might go the same way as the others?'

Giampiero laughed. 'I took out some insurance policies of my own. First, I absolutely refused to change my will in her favour. Then, on the excuse that no company would offer me cover with my record, I made certain that I was of more use to her alive than dead.

'After that I began sowing ideas into her head. Other possible ways of screwing me for the money. Moving in the circles she did she had accumulated certain contacts. Connections with the fringe of the Mafia, people who would do anything provided the price was right.'

Monsieur Pamplemousse signalled for some more coffee. His own had gone cold. 'And the price?'

'They would keep half the money extorted from

me. The rest would find its way back to her. After that she would disappear out of my life.

'It looked all too easy in the beginning. The head was meant as a preliminary salvo; a warning of what was to come. It was a reasonable replica of my own. It ought to have been—I happen to know the man who made it; he is one of the best. The arrangement was that at the appointed time I would be sitting at that particular table—by the entrance. The people carrying out the operation were far removed from those who organised it and had never seen me. Afterwards there would have been a note demanding money. A large sum.

'You can imagine her reaction when she was refused the table. Eva was not used to her requests being refused.

'She always got what she wanted. When she discovered that you had actually ordered the same dish—not all that surprising in view of the fact that it is a speciality—she was almost beside herself with rage.

'What was even worse from her point of view was that the people carrying out the task had by then got it fixed in their minds that you were the right target. Hence the second warning up on the hill the following morning. By then she was beginning to panic. She needed to contact them but didn't know how. She needed time to put matters right and time was the one thing she didn't have. That was when she tried to get you out of the way for a while by sawing through your balcony rail. One way and another you were a bit of a problem all round—from our point of view as well as hers. The local police had to be warned from on high not to be too interested.'

Monsieur Pamplemousse mulled this matter over in his mind. He wondered what would have happened if he'd agreed to take another table that first night. Perhaps that was what life was all about; choosing the right table—or the wrong one—whichever way one looked at it.

'What I still don't understand,' he said at last, 'is why I didn't receive any demand notes. What went wrong?'

Giampiero smiled again. 'They were addressed to me. I have them still. I tried to warn you to be on your guard, beyond that . . .'

It was said in exactly the same tone of voice as had been used for the rest of the story. Monsieur Pamplemousse felt a chill as he realised how narrow his escape had been.

How could anyone be so matter-of-fact about someone else's life? Then he shrugged. Every man to his job. There was a time when he might well have acted in the same way.

'I still find it incredible that you should carry off the charade of the false hands for so long and get away with it.'

'Any more incredible than making people believe you have two false legs? I must say I believed that myself for a while. I felt very sorry for you.'

Giampiero had an answer to everything.

'Besides, people tend to turn away from the abnormal. They don't want to embarrass you. As far as Eva was concerned it was never an *affaire d'amour*. She was only too pleased to leave the *consommation* of our *mariage* until later. Sex was not her prime motivation. And although she didn't know it, the marriage wasn't for real anyway. The "priest" was from Interpol—the best man and all the other guests were from the office.'

Again there was a silence as Monsieur Pamplemousse digested the facts. He glanced around the square. The *boules* game was already under way. The window in the outfitter's was in place. He looked up towards the mountains and thought of Doucette. Perhaps he would buy her a gazebo when they got back to Paris. He could stand it on their roof garden. Except that the sun would never be that strong. She would probably demand an electric fire. That would mean running a lead up. It was typical that she should take to it in such a bizarre way. Typical, also, that she had put the fear of God into her captors. They probably still didn't know what had hit them. He hoped she was all right up there.

'I shouldn't worry.' Giampiero broke into his thoughts. 'They won't come back.'

'Shouldn't you be chasing after them?'

Giampiero shrugged. 'That is for others to do. I have finished my part. Besides, the Mafia in my country are very predictable. The moment the heat is on a link in the chain will be broken.' He made a brief throat-cutting motion. 'Someone along the line will quietly . . . disappear. We will never reach back to those that matter. The ones at the top.

'As for Eva . . . I would not like to be in her shoes at the present moment.

'Consider the facts. She made a deal. A deal involving a great deal of money. As soon as she heard about the shooting in the hospice yesterday she left, but they will catch up with her, make no mistake.

'They have one great advantage. They know who

179

she is, but she does not know them. One evening, wherever she is, there will be a knock at the door.

'And when they catch up with her they will not let her out of their sight, not until the insurance money is paid out. And when they discover, as they will do in the fullness of time, that the money doesn't exist, they will not be pleased.

'I think we shall not hear of Eva again for a long time to come—if ever.'

Once again, the matter-of-fact tone in which it was said contrasted strangely with the life going on around them. They would go their separate ways and the ripples would die away. Working for *Le Guide*, where the biggest crime was a misprint, had its compensations.

He stood up. 'Thank you. Perhaps we shall meet again one day.'

Giampero held out his hand. 'Perhaps. It is a small world.'

'It is like my insurance on Madame Pamplemousse,' said Monsieur Pamplemousse meaningly. 'That, too, is small.'

Giampiero smiled. 'Ah, but have you ever enquired as to Madame Pamplemousse's insurance on *your* life? That is a much more pertinent matter.'

'*Bonne chance* to you, too!'

'*Ciaou!*'

The exchange was automatic but without rancour.

Monsieur Pamplemousse left and made his way back into the hotel. For a moment he toyed with the idea of going back up to his room, but there was no point. His luggage was packed, a note left for Doucette.

His goodbyes had already been said to Madame Sophie. There had been a strangely muted meeting in her room the previous evening before dinner. He'd had no wish for a repeat performance of the activities earlier in the week now that Doucette was there. But he needn't have worried—Madame Sophie had her own set of rules. It was a question of territories.

She had been all sweetness and light. She quite understood about Madame Pamplemousse and wished her well. She was lucky to have such a fine husband.

It was as if nothing had happened between them. But her farewell kiss had lingered in his mind and like a schoolboy he hadn't washed before going down to dinner.

That same evening when he and Doucette arrived back in their room there was a fresh bouquet of flowers awaiting them. Doucette had attributed it to him and he hadn't denied it for fear of sparking off a whole train of questions. For a while it had been like a honeymoon all over again. But the moment had been short-lived. There had been complaints about the missing balcony rail—someone might have got killed—disapproving sniffs arising out of the smell of stale smoke which still hung about the furnishings, implying that he'd taken up the 'habit' again; and a rather nasty scene about having to share the room with Pommes Frites.

Pommes Frites had been at his most uncooperative. When he didn't want to be moved his weight seemed to grow four-fold, as did his snores. The ones he'd given vent to that night had been among the worst Monsieur Pamplemousse had ever known; like a herd of cows suffering the after effects of a particularly bacchanalian New Year's Eve party.

Things were soon back to normal and breakfast had been taken in monastic silence. Shortly afterwards Madame Pamplemousse had left for the gazebo.

Monsieur Pamplemousse glanced into the kitchen. Auguste was supervising the removal of some plastic bags of ice cubes from a work top. He must be about to make some pastry. As he caught sight of Monsieur Pamplemousse his face lit up and he waved to him to come in.

Motioning Pommes Frites to stay where he was, Monsieur Pamplemousse entered the holy of holies.

'Forgive me.' Auguste was already hard at work, up to his wrists in flour. 'It is a large wedding and there is no one so hungry as those being given a free meal. Most of the guests will have been "saving themselves".'

Monsieur Pamplemousse watched, wondering what the secret was. Why didn't his pastry turn out like Auguste's? Why didn't Doucette's for that matter? Why didn't most people's?

'The secret?' Auguste laughed. 'There is no secret. A cold surface to work on. The pastry mix and the butter must be of exactly the same consistency. If the butter is too hard it will not roll out properly—it will go into lumps. If it is too soft it will spread. That is all. That and these . . .' He held up his finger tips. 'A lot of hard work with these.'

Perhaps, thought Monsieur Pamplemousse. But how many bothered? Life was too short for most people. Therein lay the difference between those who were just content to make pastry and those who set their sights on higher things, like a third Stock Pot.

He said his goodbyes.

'*L'année prochaine?*' Auguste looked at him enquiringly.

'*L'année prochaine.*' Something inside him made him add, '*Bonne chance,*' in a tone of voice which he hoped embraced all that had happened during his stay.

Auguste smiled. 'Life goes on. If you are a thinker, then it makes you laugh; if you "feel" then it becomes a tragedy. Me?' He lifted up the dough with both hands. 'Me, I am happy with my pastry!'

His luggage was waiting for him in the hall. He paid his bill and asked for Madame Pamplemousse's to be sent on.

Madame Sophie was still busy in the dining room. There had been another delivery from the *fleuriste*. She blew him a kiss with her eyes.

'*L'année prochaine?*'

'*Oui, l'année prochaine.*' He'd keep his door double-locked next time. Or would he? Perhaps it would not be necessary.

The chambermaid carried his bags for him through to the back of the hotel where his car was parked. Her nose was held high in a permanent sniff. The bare patch of lawn marking the spot where the gazebo had been stood out like a sore thumb. He opened the car boot and felt in his pocket for some change while the maid bent over to put the bags in. Even her backside looked disapproving.

Suddenly, the sight of her skirts riding up over her buttocks proved irresistible. He did something he had never done before. He reached over and gave her a pinch. Her behind felt hard and un-yielding.

The effect was instantaneous, if not entirely satisfactory; the sting from her hand extremely painful. The only consolation was that he'd saved himself ten francs. Pommes Frites obviously didn't know quite what to make of it all as he clambered in on the passenger's side and made himself comfortable.

The engine started immediately. He must change his battery more often.

As he backed the car to turn out of the hotel he realised someone was watching him from the shadows. Inevitably it was Inspector Banyuls. He must have witnessed the whole episode.

Inspector Banyuls undoubtedly had witnessed it. As Monsieur Pamplemousse came to a halt by the gate he leaned through the window.

'Incredible!' His breath was stale as though he hadn't slept for several nights. 'Tell me, how do you do it? A man of your age.'

Monsieur Pamplemousse thought for a moment and then, remembering something, reached for a small phial on the parcel shelf. He removed the top and shook a dozen or so pills into the inspector's hand. 'Take three or four of these before you go to bed tonight. You'll find they will work wonders.'

Inspector Banyuls was too surprised to refuse. He stammered his thanks as the car moved off. 'You are more than kind. I won't forget.'

'No, I'm sure you won't!' Feeling an unwinking gaze emanating from the passenger side, Monsieur Pamplemousse shifted uneasily in his seat. He wondered if he'd been over-generous. They *were* Pommes Frites' pills, after all. Travelling about played havoc with one's 'systems' and they were really kept for emergency use in case of constipation. Touch wood, he'd only had to use them once.

In Le Touquet. As he remembered it, half a tablet had been more than sufficient. Inspector Banyuls was due for another sleepless night.

He took a last look round the square. As they drove past the office of the P.T.T. he wondered how long it would be before his parcel reached Paris.

It would have been nice to have stayed for lunch, but with a wedding breakfast going on the service would have been stretched. Besides, he had to make Rouen by Sunday. Ideally, that meant Clermont Ferrand by nightfall. If he went over the top by the Route Napoleon it would take longer than cutting across to Orange and the *autoroute*—it always did. But the weather was good, the sky blue and clear. It was an ideal day. He hadn't known it quite so good before. Sometimes he'd gone that way and once up the mountains he could have been anywhere. When the cloud was low it was a waste of time.

A little way out of town he pulled into a small lay-by—a pimple on the side of the road which had been hacked into the hillside.

He looked back down towards St. Castille, nestling snugly in the valley. Through his binoculars he could see the square. Cars were beginning to arrive at the hotel. He glanced at his watch. Twelve thirty. The pace would be quickening imperceptibly. Felix would be at his place making sure all was well. Sophie would be welcoming the guests. Conversation would have stopped for the time being in the kitchen.

He wondered what his verdict should be on La Langoustine. Was it ready for a third Stock Pot? Was *Auguste* ready for it? Without a shadow of a

185

doubt he should retain his second. But there were other considerations. Undoubtedly a third would change the lives of the Douards. Perhaps that was what Sophie needed. Another challenge. They would have to take on more staff. Prices would rise accordingly. The clientele would change. It was something he, personally, would regret, but he must not allow that aspect to colour his judgment.

One thing he knew for sure, Pommes Frites was ready for his lunch. Pommes Frites wasn't all that keen on views—especially when he was hungry. As far as Pommes Frites was concerned, once you'd seen one valley, you'd seen the lot. He was getting restive.

Monsieur Pamplemousse made a mark in his note-book. He'd reached a decision. Now it was up to others. To the directeur of *Le Guide*.

He felt in the compartment beside the steering wheel and took out a small jar. It was time Pommes Frites had some vaseline rubbed on his nose. The hot weather had made it very dry. That, and all the sniffing he'd had to do over the past few days. It was something bloodhounds suffered from.

His ministrations completed, Monsieur Pamplemousse started the engine again. He would drive on a little way and look for a picnic spot. He was glad they'd decided on a picnic. Pommes Frites liked picnics and it was just the day for one.

Fastening Pommes Frites' seat belt again he pulled out into the road and took a last quick look across to the other side of the valley, towards the hills where the gazebo lay . . . it sounded like the opening words to an English song he'd once heard. How did it go? . . . Over the hills where the gazebo lay . . .

As they rounded a corner and began the steep climb he tried it out, adding a few 'toots' from the car horn for good measure.

' ... over the hills, where the gazebo lay ...
  toot! toot!
And my Doucette sits knitting all day ... toot!
  toot!
Oooooooooh, over the hills ... toot! toot!
Where seldom is heard,
A discouraging word,
For her *mari* is far, far away ... toot! toot!'

Pommes Frites wagged his tail. He liked it when his master started to sing—especially when he sounded the horn at the same time for no apparent reason. It showed that all was well with the world and that the next meal wasn't very far away.

No dog could possibly ask for more.

ABOUT THE AUTHOR

Michael Bond is the author of the beloved Paddington Bear series of books featuring that charming creature. A household name, Paddington Bear has been translated into over twenty languages.

MONSIEUR PAMPLEMOUSSE is Michael Bond's first novel for adults.